Zen City

Zen City

Eliot Fintushel

Winchester, UK
Washington, USA

First published by Zero Books, 2016
Zero Books is an imprint of John Hunt Publishing Ltd., Laurel House, Station Approach,
Alresford, Hants, SO24 9JH, UK
office1@jhpbooks.net
www.johnhuntpublishing.com
www.zero-books.net

For distributor details and how to order please visit the 'Ordering' section on our website.

ISBN: 978 1 78535 350 5
Library of Congress Control Number: 2015956009

A CIP catalogue record for this book is available from the British Library.

Design: Lee Nash

Printed and bound by CPI Group (UK) Ltd, Croydon, CR0 4YY, UK

We operate a distinctive and ethical publishing philosophy in all
areas of our business, from our global network of authors to
production and worldwide distribution.

Introduction

Epitome of the Gimlet of True Cityzen Practice
A Universal Recommendation to Sit Zen
by Anonymous

1

Hear the Voice of the City! The true Cityzen is not separate from all beings.

#

After the example of the natural world (e.g. the specialization of cells in multicellular organisms and the disappearance of cell walls in animals) people in cities, under increasing population pressure and crushing market forces, with decreasing availability of natural resources and with distribution of necessary goods hampered by regional wars, strikes, and other disruptions consequent to the intense, debilitating exploitation of the social and natural environments, were forced into ever greater specialization of function and, at the same time, intimacy, reliance on immediate neighbors, dissolving traditional interpersonal psychological and eventually even physiological borders.

Ironically, the achievement of this intimacy and integration of function depended (at first) on the solitary exercise of mind-damping practices, causing the apparent, temporary separation of "individuals" from the life of the society-at-large. It was not long, however, before hermitages gave way to monasteries as their natural development, and as the influence of the monasteries began to be felt in the wide world, exercising a powerful attractive force on the beleaguered lay people, the idea of the City, as we now understand it, began to coalesce, and in due course, as we might now say: to *hypostatize*.

2

Hear the Voice of the City! The true Cityzen is like the air, which fills the lungs of dung beetles and of dignitaries alike. He has no preferences. When a leaf flutters, he flutters. When a bird falls, he is there.

\#

With the development of *hypostatization* technology and its corollary *hypodynamic* or subliming processes, the ideal of a complete instantiation in human culture of the model of organic unity in a living creature at once became practicable. Mental components of "individuals" could be hypostatically converted into flat images for transcendental diagnosis, facilitating the selection of appropriately tractable "persons" (aggregates, component heaps) as building blocks for the City and also enabling the creation of (phantom) "persons" out of the homogenized substance of the realized City to act as the City's agents in various essential urban and interurban functions.

By hypodyning "individual" entrants, dissolving intellectual, moral, emotional, and perceptual integument along with the physical, and thus freeing components for combination with appropriate parts of "other" Cityzens, while retaining certain labels (name, classification number, DNA print) strictly *pro forma*, as an administrative convenience, the life of the City could be efficiently tended, just as, in Nature, organic life maintains itself through ingestion, digestion, and assimilation. It is, of course, crucial that name be no more than a formal convenience, for, in fact, it is largely on the basis of non-attachment to name (in all its guises) that an entrant has been allowed into the City.

3

Hear the Voice of the City! The true Cityzen yields where life presses and presses where life yields. He is in responsive communion with the life of the City. Is this not a desirable condition—to be one with all things, to feel all things from within the things themselves, and to respond freely and gener-ously? Then redouble your efforts to lose self and self-gain through the practice of sitting zen. Developing samadhi, honing the mind, damping the waves of separation and doubt, ripen and fall into the wondrous City!

Chapter One

"To enter the City you have to get rid of the idea of self-gain."

...That's what Control said. Somebody else might have let me pass. It all depends what particular guy you get. This fellow, with his yardstick spine and a voice like adding-machine tape, never took his eyes off the monitor. My pose was wasted—hands folded together in front of my crotch, chin to collarbone, feet parallel; me in the dun-brown pants and the dun-brown shirt and a face like driftwood, how could he not let me through? But all he saw were the green silhouettes on the hypostatic scanner. "Not you," he said. "You're a carrier. Step aside, please. Other people are waiting."

Never mind my Doubt Mass, the inner fury that drives men toward the City. Never mind that heaven and hell were just tinder for me, burning to get into the City, spending every waking moment trying to chew through this *Saha* world, this world of illusions. All Control wanted was a flat stat and a dumb puss.

In the old days I would have shoved him and run through, but, of course, in the old days I wouldn't have wanted to enter the City. A little woman in a coolie suit, next in line, smiled at me as she brushed by. "Do more zazen," she said. "Sit. You'll get through. Don't worry." I looked at her hypostat on the overhead monitor; it was like water in a bucket, pulsing and pooling with ambient sounds of the terminal—paper rustling, latches clicking, the fans, footsteps, bits of conversation, breathing, the occasional sizzle of some City entrant up the line being hypodyned and placed—nowhere turbid or opaque.

I stepped aside. The queue itself was a foretaste of the City, a tight quarter mile of grey immigrants, folded in on itself like a wad of paper dolls. I did a western roll over the cordon and headed for the nearest exit, with an angry guard on my tail: "Them ropes are for something, you know, hick." He was brandishing his karuna rod, his compassion stick, in a way that told me he had a couple of notches on it and didn't mind collecting a couple more.

A 'sardine' shuttle was just filling up at the gate outside. I wedged in the door as it irised shut, catching a corner of my shirt. Two padded steel slabs immediately sandwiched and stacked me, ripping my shirt, and the shuttle took off.

Good. I had a berth to myself. I couldn't move a muscle, of course, but I could smell my own smell, musk and garlic, and read at my leisure the graffiti on the shredded foam around me: "YOU'RE NOT ME." Someone must have scraped it there during a long run with a pin between his teeth. I read it over and over, rather than do zazen—"YOU'RE NOT ME. YOU'RE NOT ME. YOU'RE NOT ME. YOU'RE NOT ME."—as the shuttle burrowed through the suburbs and closed in on the hick frontier.

You always feel like a transcat's turd when the 'sardine' shuttle peels you out of your slabs, lays you onto the exit belt, and pushes you out the rear iris. Doesn't it grunt as well? Or is that me?

Thin and strong, Angela was waiting for me at the hick terminal. She was wearing a patchwork she'd fashioned from scavenged fabric and stolen hankies. It was wound around her legs and torso like a mummy's sheet. She sat on a sun-bleached bench, feeding crows. "I knew you'd be back. I never even packed a lunch."

"Leave me alone," I said. She looked hurt. Let her. I walked on past her.

"Hey wait up," she said. I heard crows' wings flapping. "Don't be like that. Hell, I been waiting for you. I been doing zazen here for six hours or something. Come on, Big Man, be good to me. How about it?"

I kept on walking, like everybody else coming from the

terminal, fanning out into the hicks, into the spalled lots and broken streets, like drops of water shaken off a dog. Angela tramped after me all the way to the Old On Ramp and the Blue Plymouth Hotel, where Pirate was cooking up couch-grass seeds over a fire he'd made in the trunk. The air around him was hazy black with the kind of flimsy, sticky ash that comes from a plastic fire; God only knows what Pirate was using for fuel.

Pirate was a big, skinny guy who used to be a big, fat guy before all the ag rights went to the City. He let his hair curl out like a black sunburst, like a mane. I don't shave my head like some vanny zealots, but I keep it short, and I shave my face. Maybe that's for Control, or maybe it's a memorial for Janus, who thought I was good-looking, despite my club of a nose—symmetrical and slick, said she—and made me shave and comb.

Pirate didn't sit. He was smart, and he liked to eat. He'd practically had a hydroponic vegetable garden put together on the bed of the Red Dodge Half-Ton Hotel, when the ag cops got wind of it and declared eminent domain by the Enclosure Acts of '07. They compensated him with four cases of Circenses.

("What gets me," he'd said, chugging a can of Circenses, "what gets me is that they don't even taste any of the goods they pull in from the hicks. It's all pulverized together and intravened to the slickers. You couldn't pay me to live in the City.")

The Lincoln Continental Inn, like all the other hick dwellings, was in the same spot it had occupied during the Big Jam, when the traffic had stopped a decade before. The crew there was getting drunker year by year. They were singing and dancing with some Mack Truck stiffs, while the ladies from the Two-Tone Toyota Corolla Hotel and their pals at the adjoining Chevelle House coaxed an old tune from a peened oil drum and some junked windshields. It was tasty, and the sunset was too, like a rim of fire tickling the bottoms of the clouds, with the mountains all round for kindling.

"You can't eat that shit," I told Pirate. For days now he'd been threshing thickets of grass over a sack.

"Back already?" he said. "Couldn't get in, huh, Big Man? Too much ego, am I right? Well, Angela here'll be happy, but you're gonna have to deal with the guy I said could have your back seat."

"No sweat. Let's dance."

"Go dance with Angela. I want to see if I can get something digestible out of this. Hell, the clover was good, wasn't it? And I didn't see you choking on the bulrushes or the arrowroot, buddy. I'm a goddam culinary genius, you asshole."

Angela grinned. I shrugged. We strolled over to the Continental and started to dance. Angela tugged me by the hand. "Be nice to me, Big Man."

"Let's just have a good time, all right? I don't want to think about a thing." I pulled her up close, and we rubbed bellies, shaking and hopping with the music. Somebody put a brew in my free hand, a City issue, a Circenses; I chugged half of it and gave the other half to Angela. Some guys and gals hugged round us to dance in a big clump; then we exploded outward again, laughing.

"Big Man," somebody shouted, "we knew you'd be back. You're too crazy for the tight-ass fucking City."

The back doors of the '69 Ford Econoline Center crashed open, and half a dozen men and women in dun-brown smocks (like mine) filed out and stormed over to the Chevelle House. Some of them wore earphones, but they weren't hooked up to anything.

I stopped dancing and went over there to listen in. Angela tagged along. I could see that Pirate was making for the Chevelle as well.

"We're trying to sit," one of the van people said to the lead drummer of the Chevelles. I had seen this vanny around a lot. She'd shown up on the ramp one day and decked a couple of Mack Truck toughs who tried coming on to her: martial-arts training—I like that in a woman. I liked her freckles, too. I would have liked to count them with my tongue, but she was only interested in one thing. She was maybe twenty, but she was already some kind of honcho there, a close disciple of No Mind. She had one of those patterned Japanese cloths tied around her head—a gift from one of No Mind's visiting Jap grims—but little thickets of red hair sneaked out the sides and back. Cute little nose for a vanny zealot. "We're trying to do zazen." The drummer ignored her.

Angela jumped to the fore. "To the true practitioner, noise and silence are the same," she said. I did a double take—I did that a lot with Angela. She was always coming up with things that sounded like aphorisms from the ancient sages, but they weren't. They just bubbled out of her ad lib. How did she do it? The drummers all laughed. Pirate nodded and stuck his tongue out at the vannies.

"Look," the van woman said. "Everybody wants to get into the City. You're the same. We're the same. We need to work together, don't we?"

"Then come on and dance," one of our folks shouted.

"This year," the vanny said, "eight people have left the '69 Ford Econoline Center and been accepted directly into the City. Six more entered the City after less than a month in the Cave of the Dharma. How many of your people have gotten through?" She set her jaw and swaggered toward Angela, ready to tumble.

Another vanny woman grabbed her elbow. "Don't give way to anger, Clara. Remember what No Mind said."

"How come No Mind lives in the suburb and not in the City itself?" Pirate taunted. "How come No Mind's not a Cityzen?"

"No Mind can get in whenever he wants to," said Clara. "He's a Bodhisattva. He's been in the City and come out again. He only stays here to shepherd us through."

"Sure."

Angela said, "The true City ain't a special place. The true City is anywheres a clear heart is."

Everybody cheered. Even the drummers stopped for a moment to shout, "Yes!" I could have killed Angela, I felt so small next to her. I scowled at her and then marched straight back to the Blue Plymouth Hotel. There was a couple making out in my back seat, a hairy ape and a tough girl in overalls. "Get out," I said. "I'm back." I yanked the guy out and the girlfriend followed.

The guy kept saying, "No problem. No problem."

The girl said, "Sorry, Big Man."

I climbed in, slammed the door shut, locked it, snapped the sunshades over the windows and lay down for a snooze, but Angela came over. "Let me in, Big Man," she said. I didn't say a word. I just concentrated on my breathing. "Come on," she said. "Let me in, Big Man." I could do that. I could shut out the sound. I could breathe in and breathe out for hours, for days maybe, without anything intruding at all. "I love you, Big Man. Why do you do shit like that? Why did you run off like that? Why don't you let me in?" She started to cry. "Don't you know I'm only here for you? I guess I shouldn't say that, huh? I guess I should just do what I'm s'posta and not feel nothing, right? Well, I can't do it, Big Man."

"Shut up and go to sleep, Angela," I said.

I reached under the seat for my beeohtee. I shoved the earplug in and turned on whatever was in the player. The voice was slowing down a little, but there was still some juice in the batteries; if it ran down while Angela was hanging around I could just pretend to be listening anyway. The beeohtee that happened to be on was *Ten Days to Greater Word Power*, the last thing I'd been listening to before I split for Control. The new words were "stultify" and "harbinger." I listened to every beeohtee I could get my hands on. I traveled three days once to a battery stash I'd heard about. Before *Ten Days*, it had been *The Doors of Perception* by Aldous Huxley, *The Natural Way to Draw* by Nicolaides, and St. Augustine's *City of God*. Before that, a Zane

Gray, I think.

The passenger-side front door opened up and Pirate's tattooed belly shoved in. "Excuse me, Angela," he said sweetly. He sidled in past her, shut the door in her face, and locked it again. "I've had it," Pirate said, settling down on his side in fetal position with his head behind the steering wheel. "I'm done with today. That's enough. I bloodied those little fuckers, Big Man. I thought it would feel good, but it doesn't. It feels like shit. I'm going to sleep. Do you hear me, Big Man? I said, I'm going to sleep."

"I hear you, Pirate," I said at last. Angela had finally gone away. I put the beeohtee back under the seat. "You know what? I'm getting into the goddam City, Pirate. I'm getting in, and you're going to help me."

"Dream on," he said. "Hey, what the hell is it with you and Angela, anyway? She's a prize, man."

"Yeah, she's a prize. I'm not."

"What the hell are you talking about, a guy like you? You're buff, you're smart, you know the road, and you read all the books."

I shouldn't have said what I said then. I was tired, and Pirate was laying me open like a mother's kiss, making me feel like spilling it all. "I read them," I said, "but I'm still on the wrong side of the City line, Pirate. Nobody out here is worth shit."

"Me included, I suppose."

"You know what I mean."

"Angela's out here too, Big Man."

"She doesn't have to be."

"What?"

"Something's going on with her, Pirate. She understands too much. She's too quick."

"She talks like a guttersnipe."

"It's an act."

"You're crazy."

"Where did she used to go when she left my bed at night? How stupid does she think I am, tell me that? Were you the one messing around with her?"

"Number One," said Pirate, "you're not mad about me taking Angela—which, by the way, I'm not. That's a cover. What your real beef is, I wish I knew."

"Right. Fuck you. What's Number Two?"

Pirate shook out his black mane and yawned. "Did I have a Number Two?"

"Why else have Number One?"

"OK, Number Two: I'm going to sleep." In a minute, he was snoring.

* * *

When you can't get in through the front door, you try the back.

The moon had been waning, a thin crescent, when I entered the Cave of the Dharma, coaxing Pirate along. Now it was nearly full: I dared to peek up now and then during ritual processions near the mouth of the cave.

During zazen, my back was straight, my eyes half-closed. My legs were crossed tight, right foot on the left thigh, left foot on the right thigh—perfect full lotus and nothing but. My thumbs touched lightly at the level of my navel, my palms one on the other a hand's span below. Guys to the right and left of me, some of them Econoline grads, scratched and wheezed and whimpered—not me though. My samadhi, my zazen concentration, can't be beat. My only problem was the zendors. Like hooded snakes in their cauls and black robes, a couple were gunning for me with big "encouragement sticks" as I sat with the other City applicants, facing the wall.

They didn't use hypostat scanners at the Cave of the Dharma; everything was up to the zendors. If a zendor thought you needed a whack to get you going or to slow you down, there was no court of appeals. You took it because you knew it was the only way you'd ever get into the City. Otherwise, you wouldn't be there in the first place. Of course, the same thing goes for the zendors themselves; you understand, they weren't in the City yet either.

#

Though my skin shrivel and turn to dust,
Bones crumbling, blood run dry,
I will sit zen, past self and gain,
To wake past death into the wondrous
City.
#

...That's what we chanted every day, as the zendors carted off the three classes of the incapacitated: the dead, the ill, and the enlightened. Only the enlightened got to enter the City; they were revived and bused over to Control. The dead, the starved, and those struck too hard, too often, or in the wrong place by zealous zendors, or squeezed to death by their own frantic aspiration, were carried to the bone yard. They were heaped into pits full of skeletons and rotted clean under their boulder lids. I don't know where the sick ones went.

I'm big, but I bleed easily. My robe was already stiff with blood around the shoulders and neck where the stick had landed. Every time a zendor rounded the corner, moving away from us into the next aisle of sitters, Pirate leaned over a little and whispered something nasty. Here's a grab bag of Pirate's observations on the zendors, the "teeth and talons" of the Cave of the Dharma, the City's purgatory, set in the mountain rim of the City, on the far side of the circle of mountains from Control's entry terminal:

#

"Fuck them."

"Fucker got more nerve than Nirvana, see if I don't tear off his whack arm and enlighten him with it next time he heave ho me."

"Big Man, I must love you because if I didn't, both you and that windmill behind me would be dead and me back in the sun and couch grass."

And my favorite: "I wish that asshole would quit trying to tenderize me. I don't want to be part of your City ground round."

#

"Yes, you do want it," I whispered. "You know as well as I do that nobody's really alive outside the City. The best of us is a zed to them. We can't do what the Cityzens do. We drag thoughts like seaweed on a sinker. In the City, man, they've got no self, no sinker. They're free."

WHACK, WHACK! WHACK, WHACK!

"Fuck 'em."

We worked meal time just the way I planned. When the zendors came round with their buckets of grits and weak tea, Pirate and I begged off in the ritual manner by inverting our nested wooden bowls. We raised our shoulders to be excused to pee.

Beyond the stalagmites separating the latrine from the sitting area, Pirate and I were alone. Nobody else, zendors included, would skip a meal when there was so little else to amuse one.

"Make it quick," Pirate snarled. "I can't keep up a flow for long."

"Nobody's listening," I said. "Have you seen anything?"

"Yeah, Big Man. The wall."

"There's a way in, Pirate. I know there is. There's a secret way from the Cave of the Dharma."

"How do you know that, Big Man?"

"Angela. When we were doing it, back when, she said it once.

She knows things, Pirate. Maybe she's slept with a zendor."

"So how come she isn't here instead of me?"

"I don't want Angela," I said.

"Say, even if there was a back door, what good would it do you if you weren't hypodyned? Don't you know, man, the City is a soup? My man wants to strut in with his pecs and his quads, his bones and his blues, and his bedroll on his back, but nobody in the City takes up a square inch. Nobody's got his own liver, Big Man. Nobody's got a name. They all get hypodyned at the Control door, and then they're purely jazz."

I said, "You're wrong, that's all."

"Well," he said, "I didn't see any secret door. You can piss here till the crows come. I'm done." He walked back to the rows of sitting cushions to catch the last scoop of grits.

The Cave of the Dharma was old. It had been used for thousands of years. Long before the City, pilgrims had come to sit zazen in these dim recesses. The niches in the rock that now held electric lights on rheostats once contained kerosene lamps, and before that, candles, and before that, rags soaked in meat drippings. Way back then, people were starting to conceive of the City; they knew they had to be alone to damp out the mind waves and get rid of the idea of self-gain—like I couldn't do.

I squatted and made a face to buy time in case any zendor was looking. Another City applicant, a bald Econo guy, a late-comer with whiskers so thick they almost looked like a false beard, had joined me in the pissoir but was standing far away and paying no attention. For the jillionth time, I flooded all my samadhi power into the rock walls of the cave, scouring the surface with my mind, feeling all the jags and crevices: nothing.

Well, one thing. Useless, on a broad stalagmite, above a cracked pool of urine crystals, there was an inscription contrived to look like an ecstatic piece of zen graffiti; actually, it was an officially sanctioned pep talk excerpted from an old text of the Western Canon—"Epitome of The Gimlet of True Cityzen

Practice, A Universal Recommendation to Sit Zen." The writing spiraled around the stalagmite. I knew what it said; Angela knew the whole "Gimlet" and used to recite it to me:

\#

The true Cityzen is not separate from all beings.

The true Cityzen is like the air, which fills the lungs of dung beetles and of dignitaries alike. He has no preferences. When a leaf flutters, he flutters. When a bird falls, he is there.

The true Cityzen yields where life presses and presses where life yields. He is in responsive communion with the life of the City. Is this not a desirable condition—to be one with all things, to feel all things from within the things themselves, and to respond freely and generously? Then redouble your efforts to lose self and self-gain through the practice of sitting zen. Developing samadhi, honing the mind, damping the waves of separation and doubt, ripen and fall into the wondrous City!

\#

The guy who first wrote that, I could have arm-wrestled him right through the table. I could have out-thought, out-felt, and out-sat him. But he was probably a Cityzen now, and I was still a hick. Discretely, eyes down, hands folded together in front of my solar plexus, I made my way to the stalagmite. Maybe it was hinged. Maybe it was loaded. Maybe it opened or slid, rose up or drilled down—"*...fall into the wondrous City!*"—carrying a person with it. I sneaked behind the stalagmite, out of the stick men's line of sight. I hugged the hard, damp thing, pushing, pulling, lifting, jamming: nothing.

Nose and forehead on cold rock, I could see, barely in focus, the piece of inscription in front of my face: "*...fall into the wondrous City!*" I was an idiot. There was no goddam back door. I had to do zazen.

I gritted my teeth and charged back to the sitting line. The bearded Econo fell in behind me. The meal had just ended and a horsewhip was being snapped to begin the next round of sitting. "Go home," I whispered to Pirate before the zendor came around. "I don't need you. I'm gonna *sit* my way in."

"Suit yourself, asshole." He started to get up, but the zendor was there. *WHACK, WHACK! WHACK, WHACK!* I heard the stick slam down on Pirate's shoulders—"Shit."—then the zendor's footsteps closing in behind me, and the stick:

TAP, TAP! TAP ... tap?

I swung around on my cushion. "Angela!"

Chapter Two

"Shush," she said. "Face the wall." I faced the wall. Angela laid her hands on my shoulders, as zendors sometimes did to gauge physical tension, to steady an overly ardent zen, or to make the stick wounds hurt more. "I love you, Big Man," she whispered, "whether you believe me or not. I'm gonna get you to the City."

"Hey, Angela," Pirate said, "how'd that stick fall into your hand?" It was part of an old joke, a straight line from kerosene-lamp days when one sitter tested another's progress in getting rid of ego.

Angela whacked Pirate again—that was the correct punch line.

"Ouch!" Not bad either.

I heard another zendor stomping down the aisle, a hefty one from the grunts he made as he stalked us, and from the sickening thud of his stick. Angela whispered to me, "Put your head down in your lap."

Then I heard her say to the big guy, "This one's ill. I'm taking him out for a while."

"Okay," the man said. "Is there anything you want me to do?"

"No," said Angela. "This other one is gonna help me move him." From the corner of my eye, I saw Angela lay a hand on Pirate's head.

"Okay," the big guy said. "Whatever you say." I heard him move away down the row—*WHACK, WHACK! WHACK, WHACK! WHACK, WHACK! WHACK, WHACK!*—and I heard all the sitters bending their screams of pain into pious outbursts: "No self! No gain! Naaaaaah!"

"Get up," Angela told Pirate. "Help me carry Big Man over to the old candle room. Big Man, you just hang your arms round our shoulders and breathe slow."

"She loves you all right," Pirate told me. "Damn me, but I

must love you too."

"Hush."

"Fuck, I didn't think I did, but here I am forty miles from the Blue Plymouth Hotel, letting my couch grass rot and doing what skinny Angela tells me. I can't believe it."

"Hush, you," Angela said, "please."

She and Pirate lifted me up by the armpits and walked me to the perfect, cubical chamber hewn into the mountainside in ancient days from the main passage of the cave. The room housed candles, censers, wrought-iron snuffers with Buddha figures on the handles, the abbot's pyx, the sexton's staves, scrolls and ornaments for special holidays, and other ritual implements—along with wash rags and buckets.

"How'd you get a black robe, Angela?" Pirate wanted to know. "What did you do, sleep with Control?"

"Yeah"—pulling back her caul—"I sleep with Control. Just sit tight for a minute."

"What are you doing this for, Angela?" I said. "You don't love me."

"Give it a rest, Big Man," Pirate said. "She wants to help you. What is it with you, anyway?"

Angela ignored us. Soundlessly, she opened an ancient red-lacquered cabinet and pulled out nine small, green jars, all of them the same, and laid them side by side on a smooth stone counter. Then she carefully closed the cabinet, turning the knob slightly as it came flush with the casement, so that it made no sound at all.

Angela handed us each three of the jars and kept three for herself. "Take off your robes," she said. "Smear this all over you. Please don't waste any time."

Pirate couldn't help flashing his tattoo at me, the eight-spoked Wheel of the Dharma, the symbol of the City, around his navel. He could make it shimmy and wave by undulating his stomach. I think he had put it there when he was fourteen and a zealot;

then, a dozen years later—I don't know why—he'd turned around. He had gotten some drunk with a knife and ink to add these words around the circumference: "PARTY DOWN."

"Let me do you," Pirate said to Angela as she slipped off her black robe. I jabbed him with my elbow. "What's the beef?" he said. "*She doesn't love you.*"

It smelled like eucalyptus. "The zendors use it for their sore stick hands," Angela said. "But it'll work as a lubricant, see? Use a lot. Don't be skimpy. We gotta squeeze through some tight places."

I peeled and slathered. I had to work carefully around the raw bruises on my shoulders and neck. When I winced, Angela gave me one of her concerned looks. She was about to help me, but I stopped her. "So you really do know a way in," I said. "I gotta hand it to you, Angela. You've got your finger in a lot of pies. So how come you're not a Cityzen?"

"Don't make a mess," she said, looking away. Suddenly Angela paused, still as a stalagmite or a startled deer. "Someone's nearby." We stopped moving. I didn't hear anything.

"It's okay," she said after a minute had passed. "It don't matter. It's not a zendor, and there's nothin' we can do about it without gettin' ourselves nabbed. Finish up." She slipped out of the chamber and stood outside to hurry us along.

"Wait a minute," I said. "We'll need a lamp."

"Come on, Big Man," Pirate said, falling in after Angela.

"How we gonna see?" I said. "She's nuts, Pirate. I don't know what she's trying to prove."

We followed her along the smooth flowstone leading back into the cavern. We stayed close to the wall. The stone underfoot was scalloped, and the scallops were filled with mud, and the mud hid pebbles and gravel that stuck between our toes. I had to hop to keep up while I pulled bits of shell out of my instep.

"Steady, Big Man," Pirate cracked. "It's good for your zazen."

When I tried to swipe him, I fell. Angela stopped while I got to my feet. I was covered with cave now, and stinking of guano. When she saw I was alive, she started moving again.

The guano got thicker underfoot. Lifting our legs out of it, step by step—and flicking off millipedes—became a serious project, until the pitch sloped down sharply and we were knee-deep in reeking, soupy water. It was alive with tiny white worms.

I had checked this way out before. I had been wearing boots then, and traversing a dry, narrow ledge along one wall that was not navigable by bare, tender feet. There was nothing at the end but a dripstone curtain, waves of columns thin as straw, fused together. There were gaps big enough for pale beetles, blood-sucking flies, worms and slugs to slime through, but not a human being. When Pirate and I reached it, Angela was gone.

Clusters of tiny grey bats hung from the rock dome at the edge of the light, a living ceiling of eyes, teeth, tongues, and folded, furry leather that rained urine down on us along with mites and feces. Is that how it would be when the crows came? "Come on. I'm going back," I said. "I know how to sit. I don't need this."

"Go by yourself," Pirate said. "She's got me interested. I'm sticking with the lady." Most of the time, you don't really see your friends, the real ones, the fast buddies who've held you while you shake and cry. They're like your own body—you don't have to look, just answer grip for grip, a hand up or a shoulder to their shoulder. That's what it was for me with Pirate until he said that. Dark as it was, I looked at the man. I had never noticed what an ugly mouth he had; I could hardly believe I'd ever trusted that mouth.

I heard a ghost splashing toward us on the far side of the stone drapery, but I couldn't see a thing. Then Angela's voice: "Hurry up. Duck under." Pirate laughed and dived in. A minute later I heard him surface on the other side. He stuck his forefinger through a chink in the curtain and curled it to call me along.

I thought of the City, of the purity and rest and goodness of the City, of the innocence of its zens, the elect, the completed, those with nothing further to accomplish. And I dived into the teeming pool of shit. Worms and water filled my ears, dark, grainy, brown water, quiet except for the rumble of my own blood and the humming of my own spine. I felt an opening underneath, like a row of broken teeth, and I wriggled through, emerging beside Pirate, who kissed me loudly on the mouth. On the other side of the curtain, the side we'd come from, bats fell into the dark air, thickening and swirling, or else my eyes were closed, and it was me.

Somewhere up ahead Angela whispered, "C'mon. Keep movin'," and I felt as if I were in her throat, the way her voice came up at me from the water and the walls. We sloshed forward, naked, into the dark. The unguent held to our skin, and as the water receded, the eucalyptus smell took over from the ammonia of the bats' piss and the stink of decaying guano and mite-infested silt.

"Someone's following us," Pirate said. "I hear him. Angela was right." But I couldn't tell what sound came from where.

My sense is sight, and it was nearly pitch dark. The passage rose away from the slime and narrowed until I could stretch my arms to support myself all around and above. It was still smooth flowstone, slick as a whale's throat. What light there was diminished steadily as the cave narrowed, farther from the zendo. It was hard to imagine that there was a full moon outside.

Then the passage took an abrupt turn, and we were bathed in soft, greenish light. Angela was right there. I bumped into Pirate when he bumped into her. "Brush yourself off if you want to see good," she said. The light was coming from us, from the unguent. "It only shines when it's real dark. If there's even a little twinkle, it don't work. The zendors don't even know it." I didn't bother to ask her how she knew.

We pushed on, stooping more as the tube narrowed. We

crouched, then crawled, then squirmed on our sides and bellies as the passage corkscrewed down. I reached a squeeze that I could only make by twisting onto my back and shimmying down head-first. I lay there for a minute to catch my breath, my legs up high, my head below.

There were fragile, twisted rock noodles above my head— helictites—like loose handwriting scrawled on the air. Some had been broken off by Angela or Pirate or by me when I'd twisted over, if not by someone before us. There was a bubble, an enlargement in the cavity around my shoulders, so I could bend my arms and lace my fingers under my head for a pillow.

I was resting, looking up at the strings of stone in the dull green light of the unguent, when I saw something Angela and Pirate must have missed, because, being smaller than I, they would never have bothered to twist onto their backs to get through. It was a line of writing on the stone overhead, the letters made up of little, straight scratches. They were upside-down to the way I was headed and must have been scratched there by someone going in the other direction:

\#

I'M NOT YOU.

\#

The words played in my mind like a children's rag: "I'M NOT YOU-OOH! I'M NOT YOU-OOH! I'M NOT YOU-OOH!" until my head ached and I had to get away from there, as if I were squirming away from a place in my mind. Incredibly, it worked; I wormed forward, leaving the song behind to haunt that empty niche.

In another twenty feet the tube connected with a grotto the size of a railway station. The floor was four feet below the hole I was coming out of, so that I was standing on my hands for a moment before I tumbled into the room, and the full light of me, glowing green with unguent, illumined the grotto. On one side, the grotto pinched down through a sort of barrel into a keyhole-shaped opening. The keyhole led out into a passage large enough to belly through; there were gypsum needles carpeting the opening and petals of it curling out from the wall, some of them a foot long and shaped like dried, burst milkweed pods. On the other side, the grotto connected to a wide crawl space between two collapsed strata of limestone, laid out like a slant tent roof with the canvas fly just above it; only this fly was thick with dogtooth spar.

There was a third junction that I didn't see until my leg was swallowed into it, yanked by the calf down into a hole near the floor. My zazen came through—I wasn't ruffled. I grabbed hold of a bulbous projection at the edge of the opening I had just come from, and I pulled up for all I was worth. Whatever was pulling me down had a dozen hands, or else there were lots of the critters gripping my leg and foot. In a minute, the muscles in my arms would be torched, and they'd be all over me. So I tried a different tack.

I kicked. Immediately, there were cries and confusion below. Some of the little hands fell away, and I was able to pull my leg out. Two small creatures were still clinging to it. They looked like rusted mufflers with the legs of an armadillo and the head of a human infant. When I grabbed one up, the other fled.

"Let go of me, hick," the one in my hand shouted. You could say I was surprised.

"You're a whaddayaget, aren't you?" I had never actually seen one before.

"Aw, why don't you hie back to the Park'n'Ride, you stupid hayseed?" It had a voice like a bullfrog choking on emery cloth. It was flailing its appendages, the pointed, armored tail curling this way and that, trying to find a balance point. I pinched the back of its scaled neck and watched it dangle.

"What are you?" I said.

"I'm not you, you asshole. That's for sure."

"Are you the one that wrote that?"

"Wrote what?"

"*What are you?*"

"Are you gonna let me go, or do I have to take you apart?"

"I'll put you down if you tell me what you are."

It stopped struggling and angled its little bald head at me, sizing me up, squinting me up and down. "Okay, Glowbug, I'm a whaddayaget, second generation. Satisfied?"

"No. Tell me what you're made of."

"You son of a bitch! Tell me what *you're* made of."

"You know what I mean."

I heard Pirate's voice echoing from up ahead. He had missed me. He was worried about me. Or maybe he just wanted me to think so. "I'm okay," I shouted. "I'll catch up." I lifted the little muffler guy so his face was a few inches from mine.

"Okay, here's the scoop," he said. "They hypostatted my mother from *Veltschmerz*, quicksilver, and aversion to light. My father was made of hypodyned genital crabs and death by water—and a touch of compassion, can't you tell? They call me Tenacity. Are you going to let me go now?"

"What is this, a nest of you guys? You live down here?"

"Naw, we just spend our summer vacations here. Are you going to put me down or what?"

"Were you trying to eat me?"

"Eat you? Don't make me sick. When Angela went by with the other guy, we were too slow to add it all up. We thought we missed our chance, you know? But then you come along, and we figure we better go for it."

"Go for what?"

"For a night-light, for the love of Pete. You're stupid, you know that? We just want some good light, that's all, and in case you hadn't noticed, you glow."

"You wanted to use me for a lamp?"

"Are you going to put me down?"

"What were you going to do, kill me?"

"Would you still glow like that even if you were dead?"

"None of your goddam business," I said. "Hey, how do you know who Angela is, anyway?"

"Put me down and I'll tell you."

"Okay. Talk."

"Put me down first."

I could catch him again. He was no bigger than my shin. I could bear-hug the lot of them to pus and rust. Sure, I put him down.

Tenacity shook the dignity back into his shoulders, a rim like a tin can's, just below his chin and ears. He pursed his baby lips, like someone who has too good a joke in mind, trying to stop the spread of a smile that had begun at the corners of his eyes. "Everybody knows Angela," he said, and he leapt up, turning a hundred-eighty degrees in midair, the way a rabbit will, to disappear into the hole again.

I stuck my head in after him, but I could hardly see a thing. There must have been a little light down there from some source I didn't know about, because my face was not glowing. "Hey, Tenacity," I said. "See? It wouldn't have worked anyway. I only glow when it's pitch dark. I'm no good to you." I heard a huffing sound, and suddenly there were twenty dream-creatures staring back at me from clumps in niches and ruts in the floor, walls and ceiling of Tenacity's hole.

I pulled my head out in a hurry, and stumbled away from there, but I still had the afterimage: Tenacity standing in the center holding a sharp, pointed dripstone like a lance. Huddled around him were creatures shaped and colored like thoughts and feelings, or so I imagined, and like garbage-bin paraphernalia. I saw: a red snake whose flared nostrils seemed to open into my own guts; two spined birds dripping corrosive brown fluid but whose wings were so sensuously curved that I began to have a hard-on; a rat that was all face, a human face, so that its every twitch and step formed a new expression; a large beetle with folded wings of lapis lazuli and hammered gold, whose hissing filled me with ideas for which I have no words—ways of flying inside things and of bearing children before one's own birth; a distributor cap with a grooved tongue that seemed to be licking my intuition, whether that makes sense or not... Then everything faded to the blue blotches and red capillary fuzz of my own eyelids inside.

Opening my eyes, I saw the junction room again, with the keyhole opening before me, the wide, slanted passage on one side, and the whaddayagets' hole on the other, still too close to my feet. I stepped farther back.

"Everybody's good for something," Tenacity shouted. "That's what the City's all about, hick. Everybody uses everybody."

"What do you know about it?" I said.

"Ask Angela."

Up ahead, Pirate was calling, "Come on, Big Man!" He was probably done screwing Angela. I ducked in through the keyhole and started down the passage, shattering gypsum flowers against my shoulders and back as I pushed along. There was somebody scrambling in the tube way behind. It was not a whaddayaget. It was a human or a large animal. I could hear it clawing and panting.

Chapter Three

It was twilight on the broken plateau of the Old On Ramp. A dull gibbous moon, like a shell seen in a tide pool, brightened as the twilight dwindled. A breeze was picking up—the faint smell of pine—and the parched grass stuttered in its cracks. The chrome doorhandles of the Blue Plymouth Hotel were no longer hot to the touch.

"Are you sure he's gone this time?" the woman said. "I didn't like it when he bounced us, Suds. And you weren't a lot of protection." She was pretty in a hard, wind-burned, Okie sort of way. She was wearing a mechanic's jumpsuit with the top half bunched down, exposing small, tan breasts, tight as muscles; her shoulder straps were tucked into the legs.

Her hair was not so business-like. She took care to preserve its light curls, curls to the left, like Buddha's, one of the thirty-two holy signs. She had never taken to zazen, but she had that. That and her Sanskrit name—Virya. *Perseverance.*

"Sure he's gone—trying to backdoor the City, the jerk. Pirate went with him. Open the door and let's get in." Suds was all whiskers, black and unkempt, hiding big lips and a chinless jaw and doing nothing for his watery eyes. He was wearing only a loincloth made of car upholstery, but over one arm he carried a pelt big enough to blanket them both. They climbed into the back seat and immediately rolled down the windows; it was still warm inside, though they knew the night would be cold. The car seat crunched under their buttocks—it was stuffed with dried chaff from Pirate's couch-grass experiment.

"I could take Big Man, you know," Suds said.

"Sure," said Virya, "when the crows come."

Suds leaned against her, pressing her down onto the seat. His chest expanded against her breasts, and they heaved there, forearm to forearm, clasping hands, lips locking, when his foot kicked against something under the seat, and someone started talking down there: "*Abject*—humiliating, wretched, despicable, contemptible. *Abject* is a power word that can boost your verbal mileage in a multitude of situations." The voice was oddly cheerful.

Virya pushed Suds away. "What's that?"

Suds reached down to pick up the voice. "In *abject* silence, the lad sat facing the corner." It was a black, plastic cassette-tape recorder/radio, an old Sears Panasonic. "*Coup de grace*—deathblow, a capping gesture. He pinned his writhing victim against the wall and then delivered the *coup de grace*." He silenced it with a random punch.

Suds whistled and shook his head. "That Big Man. Busy, busy."

"It doesn't get him in, though," Virya said.

"Smarts aren't worth shit. When I get in, it'll be because I lost myself making it with you, baby."

"You're sweet. I'm going to start doing regular zazen. That's what I'm going to do"—rubbing her nose against one shoulder—"unless I can find a shortcut. I've got some karma to work out."

"Yeah, karma. Where were we?" He took her thigh into his hand.

"Wait a minute." She clamped her hand around his wrist and pushed it away. "What else has he got there? Stick a few in and see, will you?"

Suds glared at her; he fished up a few beeohtees from the pile below the back seat, clumsily, to punish her for pushing him away. The pictures on the cases conveyed nothing to either of them, and the words were too long to struggle through. Suds removed *Ten Days to Greater Word Power*, and slapped in something else. The new one said:

#

I am called, 'I Am That I Am.' I exist, I exist, and you do not, except in so far as I breathe into you the breath of my life, and when it is withdrawn, you are no more. I revealed myself to you in the flame in

Midian, on Mount Horeb, and to men and women of the inner eye in countless other places with countless other names. I am Buddha Dharma. I am Allah. I am Ahurah Mazda. I exist when the City requires it. I am heat lightning, I am a sudden breeze, I am a bubble in a stream...

#

"Boring." Suds punched a button to silence and eject it, then found another tape.

They listened to Hesse's *Siddhartha* awhile, then to a little of Kapleau's *Three Pillars of Zen*, about how "Doubt Mass" gets you enlightened, and to a little more of a novel, Hilton's *Lost Horizon*, about a man freezing to death as he wandered about looking for a way into the City, sounded like. Those were the three on top. The next one, *Great Bible Stories* read by someone who introduced himself by the unlikely name of "Charlton Heston," had them longing for a couple of Circenses. Suds opened the Panasonic, threw that cassette out the window, put back the first one, *Ten Days to Greater Word Power*—"Considerate of you," Virya said— and slammed the lid down, inadvertently pushing the ON switch at the same time.

"The plural of *coup de grace* is *coups de grace*." There was a crackling noise, and then the voice changed. Suds started to switch it off.

"Wait a minute. What's that?"

"It's just the battery running down, Virya."

"No, it's not. I know who that is."

"No you don't."

"Shush. Gimme."

Suds shrugged and handed her the tape recorder. Virya turned it off, waited a few seconds, and turned it on again; sometimes that seemed to bring the juice back. It worked—a little. The deep, slow voice, like a storm door on rusted hinges, picked up a little:

#

...and I won't come back, either, Big Man, not ever. I done all I'm s'posta. So if nothin' works and you don't make it in the way I'm tryin' to fix it, then maybe you'll be sittin' listenin' to this, y'see, and I want you to know somebody loves you and don't care which side of the City line you're sittin' on, even if I was never nothin' but some jazz the City was playin', nothin' but jazz...

#

A boy was leaning in through the window. "Hey, that's Angela," he said. Virya shut off the machine. Suds took a swipe at the boy and managed to cuff him on the ear as he pulled his head out.

"Who invited you, you vanny brat?"

He was about fourteen and smelled of sandalwood, the incense of choice at the '69 Ford Econoline Center. He had shaved his head—an affectation; it was not required of neophytes at the Econoline. He was not quite bringing off the austerity to which he aspired: he was densely freckled and had cheeks the color of apricots. The robe he wore was old, grease-stained from top to bottom, and much too large for him. "Jeez, I just came to tell you about the grims. That was Angela, wasn't it? Is she on a beeohtee?"

"What grims?" Suds barked.

"Japanese, lots of them, maybe a hundred, coming down Highway 90. They'll be here by morning. Was that Angela or what?"

"They'll be heading for the City," Suds said. "If they think they can hang out on the Old On Ramp, there's gonna be trouble."

"We always like the Jap grims at the Econoline. They got a lot to teach you."

"*We!*" Suds howled. "Listen to the kid. Now it's *we*. He's been there—what, a month?"

"Five weeks."

"How's your hypostat, Rinzai? Flat yet?"

The boy, Rinzai, didn't answer.

"How did you hear about the grims?" Virya asked him.

"No Mind told us."

"Hail to the chief," Suds snickered. "How did your precious No Mind find out about it?"

"TV."

"I forgot he lives in the suburb."

"No Mind said they were marching and singing," Rinzai said. Then he started to sing what the Japanese grims were singing. He lifted his knees high as if he were marching in a military parade:

\#

Though my skin shrivel and turn to dust,
Bones crumbling, blood run dry,
I will sit zen, past self and gain,
To wake past death into the wondrous
City.

\#

"I love the grims," Suds laughed. "They come, and all your vannies throw away the dead crystal sets they've been showing off—they'd be embarrassed in front of somebody with the real article. Hey, I scoop them up and make jewelry out of 'em, don't I, Virya?" Suds rolled up the window in Rinzai's face.

Rinzai ran over to Virya's window. "Play some more beeohtee. I like Angela. What did she mean, she's done all she's supposed to?"

"Shouldn't you be sitting zen over at the van, honey?" Virya asked him.

"It's break. Come on."

"I thought you weren't supposed to talk or look up."

"Come on. Play it. I'll get into the City."

Suds laughed, "He'll get in—like Big Man and Pirate, through the back door."

"Back door?" Rinzai cocked his head.

"Leave the kid alone," said Virya.

"Play some more beeohtee, Suds," said Rinzai. "I like Angela. What did she mean, she's nothing but jazz?"

"He thinks Angela is his mother," Suds cracked.

"Shut up, Suds." Virya elbowed him.

"And some Jap grim is his dad." Suds elbowed her back.

"Break's over, Rinzai." All at once, No Mind himself was standing behind him, outside the Blue Plymouth Hotel. He had a skeletal face, thin dry lips, eyes as pale as a timber wolf's.

Rinzai stood erect so suddenly that he forgot where he was and banged his head against the window casing. Neither Virya nor Suds said a word.

No Mind stood like a mountain, his feet planted shoulder-width apart, hands clasped below his navel. The square sleeves of his starched brown robe hung neatly from his forearms like cabinet doors.

"Big Man and Pirate are getting into the City a back way." Rinzai *gasshoed* to No Mind—palms pressed together, bowing from the waist. Maybe the information would excuse him.

"A back way into the City?" No Mind's eyes narrowed. "They were going to the Cave of the Dharma..." No Mind stopped as if he had suddenly become aware that he was not alone. He relaxed his face into a vanny half-smile. "Return to your seat, Rinzai. Face the wall. When the Japanese grims come, we want them to see what good sitters we are."

"Yes, teacher." Rinzai ran toward the van, where a score of brown-robed sitters were settling onto their denim cushions. They had spread tarps and rugs over the asphalt beside the van to do their meditation on.

Virya stared at No Mind. He lingered a moment: deep samadhi. Then he spied Virya looking at him, and he blinked. He shook his sleeves and walked back to the van.

* * *

No Mind threw open the back door and climbed in. "Get out, all of you." The five disciples huddled inside had been examining a seating chart for the current crop of aspirants at the Econoline Center. "I want to be alone." They filed out, heads down, and shut the doors behind them.

No Mind took his encouragement stick from the altar on the dash. He had carved it slowly in the days before he'd had any followers, before he had entered the suburb, when he was still living by himself among the trees beyond the rest area up Route 90. He held the stick close to his face to smell the linseed oil again. He sat cross-legged near the panel door and ran his fingers over the smooth grain.

Then his fingers found the row of tiny lines he had notched on the edge of the handle. "That's the time I almost got in, but I was trying too hard; the screen clouded up and they sent me back… That time someone from the On Ramp almost saw me, and I had to leave my place in the queue… That was last week—Control's mistake. I was ready then; he just didn't like something about me. He should have let me through…"

…A back way…

Then the Voice came, the inner Voice that used No Mind's body/mind for its tongue, the Voice that had startled and shaken him in the days of the trees off Route 90, the Voice that always seemed to presage enlightenment, but enlightenment never came. The Voice had taught No Mind the charter equations of the City and the modes of practice that would bring him into accord with them. It had shown him the names and forms and rituals to teach to others. It had promised him future glories.

Bobo Shin could come with his entourage of boot-licking Japanese shave-pates. He could boss No Mind around as if he held a franchise for Bobo Shin's business. But No Mind's allegiance was to the Voice, his True Nature, his Buddha Mind—

that's how No Mind thought of it. "It is time to enter the City," the Voice said. No Mind's head jerked backward, his jaw dropped open, and he fell to the floor, writhing and drooling. "There is no one more worthy than you. To dwell in the suburb is a dead end, Noble One. Do what you must, but enter the City."

No Mind's brain filled with static, as it always did afterwards. He rose. He clenched the stick in his right hand. He tore open the panel door and stormed out among the sitters. "This is no Sunday picnic. This is the Great Matter of Birth and Death. If you don't settle it now, when will you? The only thing between you and the City is you." He whirled among them, striking their shoulders and encouraging each one with a shout. No Mind's disciples fell in behind him to do the same.

* * *

Suds reached over to roll up Virya's window and then relaxed on top of her. "The only thing between you and the City is you," he laughed, mocking them.

"You're bad." She nuzzled him and bucked his pelvis on the saddle of her hips. "I'm going to get in, Sudsy. I mean it. You want it too, don't you? Don't you, Sudsy?"

A few of the beeohtees cracked under his heel as he pressed into her. Virya laughed at his clumsiness and pulled him even closer, then guided him in. "In the City, it's got to be like this all the time, Sudsy…"

Night was falling. They kissed long and hard, twining and stroking, pulsing and dancing the old dance until they had forgotten which breath belonged to whom and whether they were beginning or ending.

Chapter Four

After the night of the gibbous moon, when the grims arrived, No Mind was gone. His disciples made up some excuse, but nobody knew where he was. He had disappeared before dawn and never shown up again, not for the three rounds of zazen before the morning meal nor for the talk he usually gave after the work period.

Bobo Shin Roshi, the pilgrims' leader, was extremely upset. He was an unusually tall Japanese monk with ears like soup bowls. "Who is greeting us?" he kept demanding. "This is very unusual. I do not think this is acceptable."

Bobo Shin kept adjusting the earplug of his crystal set, trying to call attention to it. Once or twice he furrowed his brow and squinted as if to listen in, as if it were actually grounded. It irritated him to distraction that most of these hicks didn't seem to know what it was and what his wearing it meant about him, that he was in direct communication with the City.

His seven companions stirred about the van grounds in eddies of nervosity, repeating, "This is not acceptable." The Econoline sitters stayed far away, as if the visitors were charged particles of the wrong sign.

Clara, red hair and freckles, the vanny spokesman, tried making them nettle tea. "Not acceptable," Bobo Shin said. "We must speak to No Mind. The City is at peril. This is no ordinary grimage. We have been sent from above."

Bobo Shin was perplexed at the laxity of the On Ramp. Some of the girls at the Chevelle House had propositioned his monks. He himself had been offered something called a Circenses by a malodorous individual who popped a can in his face and sprayed him with fermented hops. Human fecal matter littered the On Ramp, and stinking puddles of urine seeped from under deflated tires where feral children giggled.

Clara prostrated herself before Bobo Shin Roshi, and No Mind's other disciples did the same. "Get up," he said. "This is no longer sufficient. I am not just speaking about your City. All the Cities are at peril. Is there no one I can talk to?"

Clara thought this was the prelude to a *mondo*, the sort of verbal test that used to be administered to City applicants by Control before the hypostatic scanners came into use. She responded accordingly: "No one hears Your Eminence, thou of the shaved head and the crystal set. Your Eminence speaks from Emptiness. Only those hear who have gone beyond and are at rest in the City."

When Bobo Shin yelled and slapped the heel of his hand against his forehead, Clara took it for a sign of approval. The vannies nearby nodded and smiled at one another mystically. Bobo Shin said, "You are all idiots." He addressed Clara directly: "Come inside this thing with me. You are a complete fool, but I have to give my news to someone." Pleased by the insult, which she took for praise, Clara led him into the van by the back doors. She shut them in, alone, together.

Bobo Shin sat down and crossed his legs into full lotus posture without using his hands—the first time Clara had ever seen anyone do that. He motioned for her to sit down nearby, and she settled onto her calves as gracefully as a dancer and with equal delight. Bobo Shin lowered his eyes and took a slow, deep breath, then let it out in a thin stream.

He looked up at Clara. "I am not asking you a testing question. I am not talking City talk. My butt is on the floor, my nose is between my eyes, and I am trying not to be distracted by your feminine qualities. On the other hand, I may throw up any minute from the smell of this place. Do you understand what I'm saying?"

"No."

"Is that supposed to be a zen answer?"

"No. What about my feminine qualities?"

"Never mind. Just listen. Your City has asked me through the holy crystal set to intervene in order to prevent a great catastrophe. Someone is worming into your City, someone who couldn't pass Control in an *asamkhya* of *kalpas*."

"A long time?"

"Correct. He is underground. He is inside the mountain. He is being helped by a renegade called Angela."

"Angela?!"

"You know her?"

"Only a little. She was with Big Man, but he dumped her."

"He ceased having sexual intercourse with her," Bobo Shin translated.

"Correct."

"Who is Big Man? You must bring Big Man here to talk with me."

"He's gone," said Clara.

"What?"

"Big Man left about a week ago."

"He went to the Cave of the Dharma," Bobo Shin conjectured.

"How did you know? He may have gotten into the City by now."

"Not possible."

"There was somebody else with him. A guy name of Pirate. 'Party down.'"

"I beg your pardon?"

"'Party down!' That's what it says on his stomach."

"On his stomach?"

"It's a tattoo."

"You are a complete fool. You should not have been given a position of responsibility. You will never enter the City. I need to speak to No Mind. Where is he? Is he in the suburb? He has a home there, has he not?"

"What's going on, Roshi?"

"If Big Man arrives at the City, if Angela lets him or anyone else within breathing distance of the City without going through Control, without stat or dyne, you can kiss your feminine qualities good-bye."

"My breasts? You're talking about my breasts?"

Bobo Shin uncrossed his legs and swung himself into the passenger seat. "I will not let myself be distracted," he said. "This is too important."

"Are you saying that you want me, Roshi?"

He was staring at No Mind's little altar on the dash, the incense pot, the statuette of Shakyamuni twirling a flower. "If your City is destroyed, all the Cities will be destroyed. The interurban ecology is very delicate, Clara. That is why it is so well protected."

"Do you actually find me attractive?"

He would not look away from the altar. "Yes."

She climbed into his lap and reached inside his robe.

"Wait," he said. He found the string that released the windshield shade. It unrolled from above the sun visors, where the rod was jerry-rigged, and clacked against the dash.

"I love the Japanese," Clara said, caressing the insides of his thighs. "You invented the City."

He was sitting bolt upright, as in zazen. "We understood it first," he said. "We had to. So many of us on so small an island. So much energy. So much intelligence. So many empty bellies. Please don't stop."

"I am honored."

"We should not be doing this now," Bobo Shin said. "What would any of us do without the Cities? What would there be to live for? We would all become swine, warring swine, prostitutes and trash like the shit bags outside this place. Please don't stop. I am a bad priest."

"No, you're not. You are a great teacher. You're tired. You've been walking down Route 90 all night. After you've rested, we can look for No Mind in the suburb. Then we can all go and save the City."

"Yes. Rest. Then the suburb. Then the City."

"Do you really like me?"

"Yes. I'm going to make you a teacher. You will have your own ramp, your own van... Please don't stop." He was at last starting to relax his back, curving down, tucking his pelvis up to meet her cheek as she laid her head in his lap and encircled his waist with her arms.

The Earth slowly swallowed the sun again. The moon, past first quarter, brilliant in the empty sky, shone on the West Coast mirror and glinted in over the side window shade; Clara, vacant, contented, caught it. Bobo Shin had dozed off, and Clara, bliss-fully at home in the Roshi's lap, had just lolled there and let him. What a long, hot walk it must have been, two days and a night down Route 90 from The City of The Million Buddhas, prostrating at every twenty-seventh step.

She hardly noticed Rinzai knocking at the door. Sotto voce: "Hey, Clara, aren't you ever coming out? The monks are scared even to ask. Jeez, Clara, what are you guys doing in there?"

"Shh," she said. "Shh."

Chapter Five

The full moon above, beyond his seeing, No Mind had squirreled through red silt into the lava tubes beneath the karst, mind aglow with terror. He felt lost, soaked into siphons and swallets, into dark boxwork chambers with flutes and corkscrews where eyeless beetles inched through grey-white meltwater. His senses stained and permeated them—was this death, to lose one's own body for the Earth? Gypsum and calcite, blank eyes and chitinous bellies became his skin. He bristled with mole crickets and itched with pale slugs masticating earthworms. A blind, white fish, anus frontwise behind the gills, slithered through his senses like a vagrant thought.

Then, stuck in the tube, his little human body announced itself again, separate and mortal. The Voice tried to help him. *"Push, No Mind. If you can't go forward, go back. Don't let that witch Angela get hold of you now."*

"Yes, Lord Buddha! Though my skin shrivel and turn to dust..."

"That's it, oh Noble One. Forget not your ancient vow. You must enter the City. You must follow the witch. She is icchantika, without buddha nature. The others are also icchantika. Kill them if you need to."

"Kill?"

"Their lives are like smoke, like dust, like flowers in the air. Snuff them out. Enter the City. Push, damn you!"

Behind him No Mind felt the water rising, pushing, trickling through. Ahead, there was movement—someone coming.

"Push, push, No Mind." His Voice merged with the puddles' drip and trickle. *"But if the icchantikas find you, be shrewd, Noble One. Be shrewd. Kill them all."*

* * *

If I was going to get eaten, I'd rather it started with my fists than my buns. I backed out through the keyhole and faced about to see what kind of beast was tailing me. I squinted across the grotto to where the corkscrew squeeze opened into it. Imagine my pleasure at seeing No Mind pinched in that hole.

"Doing zazen, are we?" I couldn't help myself. The tight-assed bastard stuck out, wiggling head and neck like a sardine in a cat's maw. Or, for that shaved head of his, he could have been a baby, nasty with meconium. When he lifted it, all bloody, I saw the thick tuft of hair on his Adam's apple—fake whiskers that had been scraped down his neck. So the bald, bearded vanny at the stalagmite pissoir had been No Mind. Lord, I had to laugh.

"Help me out."

I grabbed his chin and yanked. I heard his neck pop, and he yowled, afraid something had broken. I eased his chin up with two fingers, the way you'd coax a virgin's kiss, and I knelt down in the grit and putty, eyeball to eyeball with No Mind. "Gee, you're not making it through," I said. "Too much ego, must be. Sorry, Jack. See, *to enter the City, you have to get rid of the idea of self-gain.* Not you. Toodle-loo." I stood up again, squeegeed muck and drip off my knees, and started to walk away, taking my light with me.

"Big Man, wait, please."

I didn't. "It'll rain crows before I lift a finger to help you, No Mind—a Bodhi-fuckin'-sattva like you."

"God, it's dark." Tears yet.

Reminded me of Alice on my beeohtees, where she cries up a flood, then floats away in it. The muck underfoot was starting to puddle and splash. There was a breeze at my back. In front of me, down the tube, Pirate was squirming on his belly out of the keyhole. He jimmied himself out and steadied himself spread-eagle against the roof and walls the way you would in a funhouse barrel. Then he stumbled toward me, hand over hand along the stalactites, a row of thin, slanted dripstones, till he was in my face.

"Done screwing Angela?" I said.

"You never quit. What's happening back there?"

"It's No Mind. Forget it. Let's just go."

"No Mind? What's he doing in this shit hole?"

"Why don't you go ask him, Pirate? Let me through."

Shouting past me, right in my ears, damn him: "Hey, No Mind!"

No Mind stopped blubbering for a second. "Help me! Someone help me!"

Pirate started in on me in his adult-to-adult voice. "Listen, buddy, I'm none too partial to that dude either, but we can't let him rot there."

"Why?"

"Fuck it. You want to get into the City? How you going to get into the City with an attitude like that? What the hell is your goddam City about anyway, if the zens can carry around a mind like that?"

"I'm calm as can be, Pirate." The hulk of him just about corked the passage in front of me. I figured I could take him pretty easy if it came to that. The man's an ape.

"You sonuvabitch, you'd let someone die?"

"Life and death are illusions, loverboy. Get out of my way."

"What's happened to you, Big Man? Is this what zazen's done for you?"

I hadn't heard her coming, but Angela was peeking around Pirate's shoulder. "He followed us from up by the candle room, didn't he? I toldjas I heard somebody. What's goin' on?"

Pirate kept looking straight at me, and I kept looking right back. "It's No Mind. He's jammed. Big Man says let him die there."

Angela poked her head under Pirate's arm to see me better. She reached her little hand through and tried to turn my head so I'd look at her. I did it, but I burned her with these eyes, I can tell you—my samadhi power is strong, and when I send out like that, nothing can come in, nothing can touch me.

"Shame on you, Big Man"—stroking my forehead, my cheek, my lips—"you don't wanna be that way. Let's go back and git him."

We were all in a clump, the knot of us in that stone throat. I caught Pirate's eye again. "You go to hell, mister," I said. I turned around and led them back. The passage widened to a domed void where No Mind's hole ran in.

"Lookit them stone straws." Angela groped along behind. "They all slant back one way—that's how it must blow in here. But now the breeze is hittin' us the other way. Didjas notice that?"

"So what?" I said. Angela being smart again.

"So it's gettin' awful wet. I think maybe we're in trouble. It's floodin' in somewheres. Must be a storm up above. The pool under that little waterfall we come by was foamin' up with twigs and pebbles and dirt. It's drippin' in through there..." We reached No Mind, coughing and whimpering in his squeeze. He was straining to keep his chin high—muddy water gushed out under him. A wind stinking of rotten victuals sprayed it into a pretty cataract. "...And through there too."

Pirate worked past me to where No Mind choked and spat. He found a purchase with his fingers, in behind No Mind's shoulders. He twisted, eased, shimmied, and yanked. No Mind groaned, "I am not separate from all beings." His head bobbed as he gurgled and watched angels.

"I can't budge him. He's in tight."

"Let him drown," I said. "He's not separate from all beings."

No Mind rambled, "I am like air. When a leaf flutters, I flutter. When a bird falls, I am there..." Suddenly he stiffened. His face was red. He pushed and squeezed as if he were trying to shit himself out of his own sphincter.

"Push hard, man." Pirate held No Mind's head away from the stream.

"This ain't gonna work. You can't get through that way."

Angela cut in front of me and sidled up against Pirate. Pretty woman, naked as a skinned bean. "He's gonna drown like that."

"...I yield where life presses. I press where life yields" — grinding out the syllables.

Those same little hands she'd laid on my arms, Angela put them on Pirate's bare shoulders. He looked round at her, and she said, "Slap his face, Pirate, and then get out of the way."

"What?"

"Do it."

He whacked No Mind across the cheeks—"Owww!"—and scrambled out of Angela's way.

"Now wake up." Angela leaned close to the hole. The stream flowing under No Mind sprayed into her face and ran down her sides, trickling over her hips, down her thighs... "Listen up, No Mind. You got to wake yourself. Relax now. Relax. Feel that water against your belly?"

"Uh huh."

Angela lifted No Mind's head to stare him awake. "Attention, No Mind." She peered right into his eyes. His lids unclenched and lifted.

Suddenly, Angela gasped. She was still as dripstone.

I leaned in. "What is it?"

She kept her eyes fixed on No Mind's, but she acted as if nothing had happened. I knew better. I'd had her in bed, dammit. I'd been inside her.

"Relax, No Mind. Feel where your skin touches the rock. Just breathe. Let go now. Breathe out," she said.

No Mind sagged and loosened. He sighed, and suddenly he shot out of the hole like an artillery shell, knocking Angela to the ground. There was a rush of water and bad air. Pirate tumbled back against me, and I fell, knocking my head so hard it stunned me. When I hauled my butt out of the soak and silt, I saw blood through the tatters of No Mind's girded robes. His back was lacerated from dogtooth spar. Angela was struggling on the floor of the cave underneath No Mind's prone hulk. His hands gripped her throat. *He was strangling her.*

I scrambled over Pirate's carcass while he tried to scramble up over me. He hadn't seen No Mind grab Angela's throat. Reaching for No Mind, I didn't care if my knee crossed Pirate's face, but he sure as hell did, and he threw me back over before he realized what was going on. We were all over each other—and No Mind was grinding Angela into the muck.

I tried to muscle past Pirate. "No!"

All at once, the whaddayagets clanged and scrabbled down the passage. Before I saw them, I felt them coming, like blood tingling back into a pinched limb. They sloshed. Some squirmed. Some flew. Some arrived suddenly by devices that have nothing to do with travel through space—they were just there. The dropsical, spined birds swooped onto No Mind's back and clawed blood from his shoulders. Memories of snakes coiled around his legs and began to swell, pinching up flesh in scarlet ridges.

Tenacity himself clambered up to No Mind's face, wailing like a spanked baby. When the man lifted his head, Tenacity squeezed in between him and Angela. He snugged between their necks like a braced bit. His baby face swelled and reddened. Then there was a loud report—backfire—and No Mind's torso hinged up like a jack-in-the-box, flailing in a puff of brown smoke. The face-rats pinched his elbows in their dimples to make sure he didn't spring down. Angela rolled out from under.

Tenacity reared up to balance, vertical, on the point of his armadillo tail. He bellowed and spun. The chamber, chockablock with the strangest critters I'd ever seen, heard, smelled, or thought of, shook with laughter deep as a cracking glacier and high as a spine's hum. Pirate and I just stood there the best way we could, our four arms dangling at our sides. Angela looked ready to smile, only it was too much trouble just breathing.

"You dears! You sweeties!" she croaked at last. The

whaddayagets seemed to pour toward her like oil down a funnel, all rainbows, spiraling into her lap, perching on her forearms, slithering, subliming, caking around her shoulders, catching like smoke wisps in her brown hair. The heavier ones tramped or rolled along the floor, some of them underwater.

"Save it, bitch," Tenacity growled. "We just spied you running back across our hole, and we figured we'd get some light this time, that's all. So how about it?"

"That's how come you saved my life, huh?"

"That's how come."

The whaddayas laughed: japes and wisecracks circled like sparks. I kept twitching my nose to smell what they said. I had funny dreams. I felt fat. We were outside in a downpour. I had an odd number of every body part. Pirate was my mom's nose ring. Then they settled down.

"Aw shut up, you mongrels," Tenacity said, a second after they'd quieted down.

"Let me go." No Mind twisted in the face-rats' cheeks. They sucked his head into a nostril. "*Lmmgg! Lmmgg!*"

Pirate found his voice. "What are you dudes? Angela, what are they?"

I just watched. I wanted to see what kind of a fool they'd make of Pirate.

Angela chucked a little blue astigmatism under the chin. She was cuddling four or five indescribables and kissing a few tinies—they smelled like stale Circenses. They looked like glowing cigar ash. A bunch of others waited in line. I say "a bunch"—I could swear they were fifty thousand, but the cave wasn't big enough for ten. Angela seemed to know all of them. "Tell them what you guys are, Tenacity."

"Depends. Do we get the light?"

"You saved me. I guess I owe youse everything."

"Say yes or say no, you liar."

"Yes."

"Okay." Tenacity swung round to face Pirate. "Whaddayaget if you cross a mare and a donkey?"

Pirate looked at me. I shrugged. "A mule," he said.

"I figured you'd know that, you dumb hick. How about love and hate?"

"What do you mean?"

"Hypostat 'em. Make 'em into things. Mix 'em together. Then hypodyne 'em back to ideers. So whaddayaget?"

"I dunno. Ambivalence, I guess."

Tenacity pounded himself in the middle— a hollow clang. "That's one for the hick. Ambivalence, come round here, buddy."

It was Ambivalence... I think. A big guy, sort of. He danced over to Tenacity's side and took a theatrical bow, or else he stayed where he was. Pirate shook his head. "I don't get it."

"Sure you do. You're doin' great, hick. Now tell me, whaddayaget if you cross *Veltschmerz*, quicksilver, and aversion to light with genital crabs, death by water, and compassion?" Tenacity shot a mean look at me and warned, "You shut up, you big beefsteak. You know this one."

"I give up," Pirate said. "Whaddayaget?"

"Me." He spat used motor oil in Pirate's face and led the others laughing.

"You're those things. Are you those things? I heard about you. You're *whaddayas*."

"I got one more, whiz kid, when the mestizos here put a lid on it." The laughter, like sausages twisting in their skins, like the smell of the ocean, like grippe, like nostalgia, like two-and-a-half feet, then a bus or a flat stone, stopped. "Whaddayaget if you cross a man with an asshole, hick?"

"Okay—what?"

"Haw! Just another asshole, Jack. Just another asshole."

"They're whaddayagets, all right." Angela was laughing right along with them. "Them old engineers, the ones 'at dreamed up the City, the ones 'at was around when the first transcats hit, they come up with these fellers."

"With our mommas and poppas, y'mean," Tenacity bellowed.

"With their mommas and poppas, I mean. They were just figurin' out how to build the City—you know—from pieces of people all put together in one body, pieces of hearts, pieces of minds, and guts and gizmos too. All that. These guys were the first stats and dynes."

"Our mommas and poppas were, you mean."

"Yeah, that's what I mean. I'm sorry, Tenacity. Do you want me to give you the light now?"

He bowed his baby head, and Angela rubbed him all over while the other whaddayagets cooed and gossiped—and all. Angela greased him like a newborn. I was starting to warm toward her, watching that, but I didn't fall for it. She said, "It'll only work when it's pitch dark, 'City."

"The big dope told me that. Now what do you want us to do with the jerk up Countenance's nose?"

I said, "Blow it." Tenacity smiled. He gave the face-rats a nod, and they snorted No Mind out into the soup on the cave floor.

He was a mess. "What happened?"

Tenacity readied to blast the booger, but Angela shook her head. "Don't you know what you did, No Mind?"

"I was stuck back there. You helped me out. Then... no. What happened? What did I do?"

I couldn't tell if No Mind was being straight with us.

"No Mind, you almost killed me," Angela said.

"I what??"

"You don't remember?"

"I must have been half-crazy. I was stuck there for a long time. I must have lost my mind."

Pirate said, "He was wet, cold, scared as hell. Maybe he's telling the truth."

Tenacity rolled his eyes. "Haw!"

But it was hard not to believe No Mind, pathetic as he was. He didn't look to have the guts you need to be a good liar: "I must have been holding onto you the same way I held onto the rocks, Angela. Honestly, I was in such a state, crushed and half-drowned, I guess I didn't know your neck from a chockstone. I just want to get into the City. That's all I ever wanted. I heard you were helping Big Man and Pirate in, so I followed. That's the truth. Let me go with you. I'm sorry I hurt you. Please let me come along."

Angela straightened her back and took a deep breath, as if she were starting to sit zen. She was still rubbing her throat. She lowered her eyes, then suddenly raised them again and shook her head. It was just as if she'd tried to think of something but drawn a blank. She tried again, and the same thing happened.

"Please, Angela..."

"I dunno," she said finally. "Look. I don't like the way it's streamin' in here. It's maybe flooded, up the way we first come. Them squeezes fill up quick if it's rainin' hard; I don't wanna send you back into that. But I dunno, No Mind. You scrunched my tubes good. I gotta go think this over a little while. All youse stick here, Okay? Tenacity, you'll be a good host, huh? Show 'em your whaddayaget stuff. I'll be back in a little while. No Mind ain't gonna do nobody no harm with these hodags around for coppers."

Tenacity was dancing around the chamber, shining on other whaddayagets, pleased to bursting with his own light. "Hey, maybe they'll all be dead when you get back, Jello—or maybe not. Who knows? Things are just like that down here."

Jello—I mean, Angela—left us. I watched her make her way down the passage and belly into the slant. That corkscrew song drifted back to me: "I'M NOT YOU-OOH! I'M NOT YOU-OOH!" Some songs stain your mind so, they're hard to wash out.

Chapter Six

Suds didn't like it. He would open a cabinet door and there would be a big mouth in there screaming at him to shut it. Sometimes a floor board would chew him out for stepping on it—it was somebody's rib or spine, it would say.

Virya took it all in stride, reciting her personal version of the *Vihara Hrdaya Sutra* and bowing frequently:

#
The Bodhisattvas of the City live in one another's body,
Far beyond deluded thinking something oddiddy oddy oddy.
Don't be scared; you'll get there faster.
No preference—therefore, no disaster.
Deep obeisance to the City!
Om svaha da diddy diddy!
#

"Let's go back, Virya. I hate the goddam suburb. I never wanted to follow the grims in the first place. I know where there's a stash of Circenses back by the Blue Mazda Motel. I want to go home."

"*Be quiet, Charles, and eat your supper.*"

"Who said that?"

"*Who said that?*"

Suds regrouped. "Were you talking to me?"

Virya stopped bowing and turned to where she thought Suds was standing. She opened her mouth to speak—someone filled it with wet clothes, slammed it shut, dropped three coins in a slot, and walked away. There was a whirring and slapping sensation above her tongue. She took another step toward Suds, and her mouth was her own again, although one knee was snoring loudly, and she could see the backs of her eyeballs. "Bear with it, Suds. I know they're headed for the City. If we get to be Cityzens,

47

what does anything matter? Just keep your eyes on 'em."

Suds's shoulder beeped. He leaned his ear into it—white noise, then a ratchet voice: *"Stop it."*

"Sorry—stop what?"

"You're licking my lip again. Stop it."

"Sorry." He wasn't licking any lips. Suds turned to where Virya would be if there were still such a thing as adjacency. "Virya, what am I supposed to do here? My shoulder's giving me a hard time."

"Just move a little, Sudsy. It's like in basketball—zones. Wherever you are, that's who you're covering. Look." Virya waved her hand. It was as if it passed across the beam of a film projector. But the images were not patterns of light falling on Virya's hand; rather, Virya's hand was the things themselves, whatever "occupied" that space—and the occupants were changing. The middle joint of her forefinger was sunlit dust, the stubble on an old man's chin, part of a star chart, heat lightning, a jingle for a new brand of sunblock, the rest of the old man's face, then Virya's uvula glistening, and then a finger joint again. "This is the suburb, Suds. Didn't the old guys ever tell you?"

He still didn't like it. "Who listens?"

"Duck! There's Clara. She'll punch you out, boy."

Suds hissed. "If I duck, I feel like shit and soup bones. What if I turn into somebody's asshole?"

"You're you. You're you. This isn't the City, Suds. Whatever you are, you're still you. Now, duck."

They saw Clara coming through a window of the living room in which they had found themselves on entering the suburb. Whether you were on an open hill above Route 90, or outside a high barbed-wire enclosure filled with conical ceramic insulators and humming coils of colored wire, or in the clouds, or nowhere, on a vast featureless desert, or in this living room for crissakes, depended on which direction you looked. Tailing the grims, Suds and Virya had just ducked under a torn fence, and there was this ottoman, this thirty-two-inch TV screen, this mug of steaming cocoa—and clumps of dogs' hair.

Clara opened the door carefully. It was hollow core, and the neighbor's water heater was inside it, as Suds, *mirabile dictu*, could clearly see *with someone else's mind*. If she slammed it, it might rupture the cold water inlet at the bottom hinge; that would flood the hallway, which was also a parking garage and the dentist/landlord's waiting room, when it wasn't part of a cow.

Suds sensed Clara's feelings as if they were flavors of gum in his mouth. In fact, when he smacked his lips, Clara winced and wiped his saliva off her forehead; she mistook it for sweat.

Bobo Shin was close behind. "Please do not stop suddenly. I do not want to collide with you. I dislike having other people inside me—even you, rice cake... Are we there?"

"Yes, of course, Roshi," said Clara, *as Suds had known she would, since he had felt her form the words in her mind.* "Of course we're there. This must be No Mind's home. It's a question of which way to look so that we align with it."

Bobo Shin shrieked, and the six monks who had tramped right on inside his buttocks and thighs backed off, penetrating Mukan—sweet-faced, younger than the rest—who carried Rinzai on his shoulders. There was no physical shock, but Mukan fell, and Rinzai fell on top of him. They fell into an old news report, a loop continuously available for reference by suburbanites. Parts of Rinzai were the announcer's low tones. Mukan's intestines provided visual images and acted as a tweeter.

#

City Planning has declared that the special status of the suburb vis-a-vis City entry is being revoked, and that henceforth suburbers will be required to apply at Control with all other aspirants, including hicks. This development has been long anticipated, since technological advances in hypostatic and hypodynamic technology has rendered obsolete the older transcategorical simulations on which the suburb is based.

'Suburban life is absolutely crow,' a senior Planner commented today. 'When the transcats were first encountered, various attempts were made to utilize the insights we gained from that intercourse. Perhaps in our efforts to speed the process, we were too hasty in granting patents and permissions to create interpenetrating and disjoint human structures.

'Souls remaining in the suburbs just want the appearance of zens, of enlightened beings, without having to trouble themselves about its actual accomplishment. Let's face it — the suburb is not a halfway point to the City. It is its own dead end. We don't want splicing and overlapping. We want real interbeing.'

City Planning has declared that the special status of the suburb vis-a-vis City entry is being revoked, and that henceforth suburbers will be required to apply...

#

Suds, in spite of himself, felt everything Bobo Shin was thinking. Bobo Shin didn't want to look behind him to see what had happened. He was afraid to move his eyes; he had just begun to get used to the puppy wagging his esophagus. "Each of you, turn your back toward me and look out." Bobo Shin made no effort to project his voice; it was everywhere. "Scan up and down along your own radius from me. Look for No Mind."

"Don't budge, Suds," Virya whispered, crouching low — or high, or flush to the wall. "You're safe there. You're just shit and soup bones as far as they can see."

"This drives me crazy," said Suds through an orifice somewhere, he no longer knew how. "You're Thursdays! Can you believe it? You're Thursdays from the neck up."

"No. Look at the note my hip is. Thursdays fall on Wednesday mornings here. There's not enough time for Thursday to have a separate day all to itself. It makes perfect sense, Sudsy. Think about it."

"No."

Mukan and Rinzai lined up with the others, a circle facing out, like the Seven Samurai. One by one, they dropped to their haunches, nauseated by what they saw and by what they became, seeing it. Suds, feeling all their emotions plus his own disgust, struck on the tactic of reciting his entire repertoire of obscenities, A to Z, in order to keep his equilibrium.

Suds felt: Rinzai alone was unaffected. ("...*Vaginal douche bag, Wombat piss, Bloody fuckin' Xyster...*") Rinzai *knew* that No Mind wasn't there, and so he didn't look. ("...*pus-dripping Yoni, wimpy prick Zarf, Asshole...*") Rinzai let everything pass through him, like a swallet sucking down a lost river, letting it stream and dribble through gypsum and calcite, stratum after broken stratum, till it broke the surface of a deep pool under a waterfall, and broke it, and broke it, rippling outward, until he was staring up at Angela's droplet-shattered face staring down at him, through twigs and pebbles and dirt.

\#

Angela never wanted Rinzai to go to the van, but he couldn't live in Angela's gaze, could he? Nothing else was sufficient. Nothing else even began to fill the hole that Angela's gaze filled, nothing except zazen, zazen, zazen.

And he couldn't rely on Angela. She came and went like moonlight on a cloudy night. You couldn't hold the moon. She'd found him, an orphan, gobbling offal at the Rest Stops, and she let him tag along. She even taught him things—how to sleep without nightmares, how to sleep at all, how to laugh from your belly instead of your chest, how to melt into your breath at twilight. But zazen was better—it was there absolutely whenever you wanted it.

\#

("...*Bastard, Cunt, Dildo brain...*") Bobo Shin hit Rinzai over the head with a hardwood crosier he found in his sleeve. "Well, what about you? Wake up, boy. Do you see anything, you worthless pustule?" Suds felt: Bobo Shin Roshi was in a hurry to settle matters before his disorientation exploded up his puppy dog's tail in all the colors of breakfast. ("...*Elephant shit, Fuckhead, Gut bag...*")

"Nope. I didn't look."

"What?"

"It's a waste of time, Roshi. No Mind is in the Cave of the Dharma."

"How in the City do you know that?"

"Just before he disappeared, I told No Mind how Big Man and Pirate were trying to get into the City a back way. Some hicks told me. I figure, he must have followed them."

"Jizo! Shit! Why didn't you tell me this before?"

("Damn me, Virya," Suds hissed, "why didn't you figure that out? We could have skipped this hellhole and picked them up down by the Dharma Cave.")

"You didn't ask me, Roshi," said Rinzai.

"Stop laughing, you insufferable turd. Stop it. What are you laughing at?" But Rinzai could no longer be found. Rinzai was all over the room, on the television, underfoot, and in the pussy cat's teeth. "Let's get out of here. This is completely unacceptable in every way. Don't bow. Don't say anything. Just go. Someone help me up, for Amitabha's sake. I am your teacher, you ingrates."

Suds felt: it took all the grims' will power and concentration, their *joriki*, to locate their own limbs and propel themselves out of the suburb, helping Bobo Shin along as he leaned against Clara, moaning, his head lolling against her bosom. Bobo Shin was sweating profusely, and as the sweat dripped down, he couldn't be sure that he wasn't a lost river flowing down someone's swallet, down, down, flowing and pooling, then reflecting.

Suds felt Rinzai watch Bobo Shin, Clara, and the monks leave the suburb. Mukan looked back before he melted out of Rinzai's view into a blinding haze of white light. Moving mere inches this way and that, Rinzai wandered about the living room, in and out of epochs and lives like currents of cool water in a spring pond. He felt something lying on the floor under his left foot, and he picked it up to examine it.

Suds whined. "My nose!"

Rinzai didn't hear that. It looked to him like a crystal set. No Mind's *chop*, his personal insignia, was stamped on the spool in red ink. So No Mind had a crystal set, his own secret crystal set. Rinzai put the plug in his ear and grounded the wire on a water pipe.

"Ouch!" Virya took the wire into her mouth. She let Rinzai twine it around one incisor.

Suds felt: the Voice filled Rinzai's mind. *"You will not have to wear this receiver again."* Rinzai's brain felt like iron molecules, magnetized, aligning to the Voice, the City's Voice. *"If you wish to wear it as a sign of rank, if it will help you to do the City's work, then wear it. No Mind will have no further need of it."*

Suds stopped his ears, then his navel, then his nose, then someone else's nose, an animal's nose, a small, sick animal's nose, a rabbit's, in fact, wet and quivering, but he still heard the Voice in Rinzai's head. The Voice was drying up the lost river, steaming away the pool and with it, Angela's image in the pool. *"I am your spine now, your buddha nature, your True Self. I will tell you where to go, Rinzai. I will tell you what to do."*

Rinzai pried out the ear plug and dropped the crystal set where he had found it. He crawled from the suburb into the white haze of the outside world. Suds felt: ghosts hobbled and tormented Rinzai. Rain poured from the steel sky in sheets. Rinzai ran after Bobo Shin, slipping in the mud, scrambling to his feet and slipping again, until he was abreast of the monks, lowering his gaze, prostrating on every twenty-seventh step, stumbling toward the Cave of the Dharma.

Then Suds was free of him. Rinzai's thoughts were gone. The monks' thoughts were gone. Suds couldn't get out of there fast enough. "That kid stuck my nose in his ear."

Virya was massaging her gums. "Come on, Suds. Get your hands off me and let's go. It's all one in the City."

Chapter Seven

Tenacity enthroned himself on the bowl of a stalagmite; it had been cratered on top by a century's slow drip. Whaddayagets crowded round him, holding appendages up to his green glow. The shadows of thoughts pulsed inside their translucent skins — they oohed. The whaddayas' sounds were like gas in a dead man's belly, whooshing and blaating, soughing and creaking.

Tenacity held forth. "City's no good. Chuck it. It's a stink hole. What does anybody want to get in for, that's what I want to know?"

"That's what *I* want to know." Pirate shook water from one foot, then the other, then the first again, when it got cold.

"You don't know diddlysquat, hick. The City is rotting, is what I'm talking about. Everybody here knows it. Chunks fall off it. *Here* is where it's at."

Big Man loosened his grip on No Mind — the winged whaddayas tightened theirs — and he leaned in toward Tenacity. "Chunks? What do you mean?"

"Chunks, hick. Bundles. Ooze. Rot. The City's got leprosy or something."

"That's a lie."

"Ooh, the hick wants to be a zen. Stay with us, hick. We're growing all the time. We're fertile as hell. We're healthy, aren't we, whaddayas?" The whaddayagets cheered. Big Man and Pirate covered their ears. No Mind tried, but the birds still pinioned his elbows. It didn't help anyway. The noise rattled from their own bowels, from the humans' as well as the whaddayagets'.

When the shouts died down, No Mind was still screaming, "Let me go."

Tenacity smiled. "Let killer go? I tell you what, while Jello's off thinking, we're going to play a little game..."

"I told you it was an accident," No Mind shouted.

"...a whaddayaget game. Right, nightmares?"

Again, the roar. This time a particular word skipped through the pandemonium: "Tag! Play tag!" The spined birds screeched it. They flexed their gorgeous wings and pulled No Mind into the air, dumping him onto a calcite shelf, a tiny balcony projecting off the chamber wall. It cracked where they dropped him, and his buttocks broke through. He perched there, terrified, exactly as if he were on a toilet. "Rules! Rules!"

Tenacity puffed blue smoke. "Sure. Rules. Okay, hicks, here's how it is. In hick tag, terra tag, dumbo, monochrome, one-note, two-D tag, the tag you're probably used to, when you touch someone, you know it; and she knows it, at the place where the two of you touch, finger to a shoulder or a butt or a heel. Same with us, only lots of us got no fingers, got no shoulders, butts or heels. What we're made of, what we're statted out of, hick, is ideers—thoughts and feelings and attitudes—get me?"

"Yeah," said Big Man.

"Okay," Pirate mumbled. Something squirmed from under his heel. Things rushed and flitted behind him. He was walking very slowly and deliberately backwards while Big Man and the whaddayagets riveted their attention on the little green god.

"Yeah. Okay." Tenacity squeezed as if his whole body were a wrinkling forehead. "Hey, beefsteak, do you feel this?"

Big Man flinched. It was as if, in a dream, his heart broke.

"Hoo boy, that must have been some love affair, huh? Still not quite over it, are we?"

"How did you do that?"

"That's what we're made of down here. We see right through you 2-D dudes just like you was tracing paper. We're stats ourselves, don't forget. So we know what feelings look like when they're flesh. Something about the way you stand, a wee tilt down at the neck bone, huh? A little quiver when you breathe a certain way. It was a tight spot in your chest. We know all about it. We see what you are as good as you see us. Even though you one-notes like to think you're sticks and mud, you're just ideers, like us."

"So?"

"So, let's play tag. If the killer can stay clean, if he don't get tagged, we'll spring him... till the crows come."

Big Man took a deep breath, massaging the adhesion in his chest, and he felt Tenacity gently disengage from the hurt inside him. Then Big Man tagged him: "You're not as mean as you pretend to be."

"*Ouch!* This bum catches on quick. I'm It."

They scattered. Pirate waded farther away down the passage, his green glow obscured from Tenacity and Big Man by scores of scrambling bodies. They were paisleys, astigmatisms, monsters and figments. To see one was to think something.

The snake that had wrapped itself around No Mind's leg slithered out of its own skin, and the skin was a voice, and the voice called: "Lust! Black lust! Blinding lust! Is that you, Sorrow?"

A small fish leapt from the gathering stream. Silvery green, horned, teeth larger than its tail, Sorrow protested, "Nobody knew that. Nobody ever saw that in me. I hate this game."

"You're It," Tenacity shrilled.

"You didn't tag me. She did."

"I don't give a damn."

The creatures fled. Sorrow splashed and flailed after them. "Worrying about something. No, nervous about women, about me, about me catching you, about whether God loves you, for the love of Mike—I can't play this damn game." He dived into the soup and disappeared.

"I'll be It," Big Man hollered.

Tenacity clanked, delighted. "Go."

Big Man grabbed the mangy arse of a flying dog. It yelped and showed its teeth—summer concerts in the park, a hundred and one strings, red wine in paper cups… "Sleepy hope. Looking for love. Am I right?"

"Are you right!" Tenacity howled. "Look at him blush. How'd you get that eye, beefsteak?"

"Zazen."

From the balcony No Mind shouted, "Wet dreams about the karst." Big Man peered up at him. No Mind had extricated himself from the hole and then stuck his head down through it to watch. "Reveries about the City glowing on its karst. Look how he holds himself—as if he were hanging from his heart."

The whaddayagets waited for Tenacity's judgment. Water rushed, wind pressed. "Smart move, hit man. The best defense is a good offense, and no tag-backs. Big Man's still It." Then to Big Man, in a whisper—"How can you dream that? You never seen the karst…"

Big Man kicked mud. "He wasn't even It when he tagged me."

"Who cares? Go," Tenacity bellowed. He sucked his head into his torso and then telescoped down to the size of a tin can top. The whaddayagets dived into the muck, flew to the ceiling, curled and squeezed behind speleothems and one another.

Big Man whirled after them, feeling his way behind their skins. Then he looked up at No Mind. There was nothing there.

Wait, no, there was something . . .

* * *

Big Man was back with the old guys, back at the On Ramp, listening to the old guys joke and prattle, showing off their artificials, swapping memories, and swilling Circenses. One geezer with a celastic chin had been on the last Mercury-based scanner probe, in the Caloris Basin. "Top that. We were scanning for transcats. The tech was good. The food ate shit. Some of the guys went forty-ten-A when we seen them things up close.

"Turns out, a guy's foot would be part of one, or their brains even,

or just the way they feel about their wife sometimes—it would be a transcat's belly. You know how them things go. That's why they call them transcategoricals. Hell, the whole mission, well, all but three days of it, was a transcat's head cold. No, I'm telling you the Buddha's truth.

"The commander, one day, somebody sets the scan on him, just for a damn lark, and there's not a damn thing there. I mean nothing. He ain't himself. No, he ain't a transcat either, exactly. I'll give you the rest of my beer if you can tell me what he was.

"No... No... No... No... Shut up then and I'll tell you. He was a transcat's turd—part—and part a diastema of another one. That's the space between a transcat's teeth. Well, that ain't a transcat, no it's not, because it's a space. You shut up. I just about went forty-ten-A. Everybody just about went forty-ten-A. That commander had to be relieved of duty. I mean, there was nobody there."

* * *

There was something in No Mind, but it wasn't him. No Mind was a moon reflecting light or a lens focusing it. Whose light was it? Who was doing No Mind? Suddenly, Big Man's stomach burned and tightened. He was about to speak...

"Suspicion. Curiosity. Paranoia," No Mind blurted out.

Sorrow leapt from the muck. "He's not playing fair. He just tagged. He can't tag again. Hell, I could win that way. Anybody could, if you can do that. This stinks, Tenacity. You let everybody get away with everything, and you don't let me get away with squat zip."

Tenacity popped from his can lid and glared at No Mind. "You're warned, killer. Are you just shooting to cover? Don't tag again till you're It." He was a can lid again, gyring and clattering into the bowl of his stalagmite.

Who was doing No Mind? Big Man looked up and saw No Mind staring at him. Big Man burned in. *What had Angela seen in*

No Mind's eyes?

From the can lid—"Play the game, oaf."

"Humble friendship," Big Man said without turning around. He had felt it through the back of his head, in Tenacity's voice.

"What?"

"You left that out, you little bugger—*Veltschmerz*, quicksilver, aversion to light, genital crabs, death by water, compassion (just a tad of that, right?), and humble friendship. That's your recipe..."

The whaddayagets' laughter was an emotional stroboscope. For one second each, Big Man experienced every feeling he was capable of. Small rock slides curtained the cave walls. No Mind fell through his hole and dangled below, hanging on by his forearms.

"Stuff it, you bloody heart murmurs." When they were still, only hiccoughs of laughter echoing from odd places, Tenacity sprang out to his full height and turned on Big Man. "You sonuvabitch, you're a ringer. Only now I'll tag you: Lost love. Wormwood. Burned your hand, now you're shy of the flame."

"Go to hell." Big Man rushed to cauterize his memory, to stem the images Tenacity had provoked, but he could not...

* * *

Forget Control's hypodyne. Forget how it chewed Janus's mind from his as a cat chews its kitten from a bloody placenta—"You will lose your small self and your name now, Janus, but you will gain the City." Think: before that! Before the last queue, where her screen had been smooth as a stone rolled by glaciers. Think: before all that, and before zazen, zazen, zazen...

Why had she left him? She was the only woman he ever called darling. Why, as they leaned toward the big picture window and Big Man kissed her neck, her breasts, her belly, had she let the moon they sighed for turn cold and black? He would forever think of that picture window when he thought of Janus. Remember the smile that sprang like a sudden flower from her lips every time he touched her, his picture-window girl.

She had left him for the City. She hadn't cared that he was from the ramps. Social barriers had dissolved when the Enclosure Acts cut nape from pate and bed from headboard fourteen years before. Ironic, that it was Big Man who had to explain all that to Janus:

"It's for the City, darling. It's all for the City. Nothing else is worth a damn. The enlightened mind sees things a whole different way from you or me. The way you and me cut things up is personal. When we say a thing stops here—'That's one thing, and over there is something else'—why, that's just our little minds making fences to keep mine from yours, don't you see?

"Even your body there—Mmmmm!—it's really full of holes. Things go in and out of us all the time: cosmic rays, germs, water, heat. Air comes in and air goes out. Food comes in and shit comes out. I go in..."—hugging her, pulling her mouth to his.

"...Not now."

"Right."

"I want you to tell me more."

He love-pecked her forehead, then each closed eye. He always smelled of gasoline, but she smelled of bath oils and wisteria. Once she told him: "Now I feel all ticklish inside whenever I smell gas."

"Sure, I'll tell you more. It's all for the City, Janus," he taught her. "For the enlightened mind, for a Cityzen, none of those boundaries exist. Do you think you'd see you and me as two people if you were a realized zen? No way."

"So why do they have to cut things up at all?" said Janus. "Why the Enclosure Acts? Why Control?"

"They see the way things really are, darling. They see the real lines between things, and that's where they put them. It looks crazy to you and me when families are split up, when towns are sectored so that three walls zigzag through your bathtub and there's a gap of sixty miles between two neighborhoods supposed to be in the same burg. Or when

somebody gets paid for somebody else's job, for Amitabha's sakes. Or when all the dates change around, and you're assigned a new father. All that stuff is training, darling. It's training us to be zens, not to be attached, to give up the idea of self-gain."

"I just love the way you can say that."

"Why don't you come down to the Old Ramp with me and listen to a few beeohtees?"

"Are you sure that's what you want to do with me?"

They made love like thunderclaps when they weren't doing zazen.

* * *

"Salvo. Lost love. Wormwood. Direct hit. Game's over. I'm the champion. Everybody cheer."

In the privacy of the uproar, Big Man edged close to Tenacity. "Tag No Mind. What do you see, Tenacity?"

"He has Voices. I can't tell if they're good or bad. Only, something's running him."

"Was he lying? Did he really try to kill Angela?"

"Who knows? Somebody's running *her* too."

"Running Angela?" Big Man cupped his ear to shut out the pandemonium. It was not sufficient—their "noise" was not just sound—but that was all he knew how to cup.

"Who cares? We love her down here. Don't you?"

"That's a one way street."

"Boy, did I tag you good," Tenacity laughed.

"How do you guys know Angela?"

"We met her when she first come out."

"First come out?"

"You know—'YOU'RE NOT ME!'... Shut up now, I gotta declare." Tenacity pinched one nostril and trumpeted steam and burnt oil out the other. "Listen up. Nobody tagged the killer. Nausea, Wizened, let him down." The spined birds ascended. No Mind could not help resisting the things, even though they meant to free him; it was instinctual—they were fierce and ugly. Nausea and Wizened overpowered him. They carried him, thrashing and biting, down to the cave floor. Then they screed off to a high ledge.

"Tantra!" A rush of airborne cinders, or of dew spiriting off a mountainside, or a dragon's breath, or rocket thrust, responded to Tenacity's call, jetting the perimeter of the domed chamber and arriving beside Big Man and Tenacity. "Fix this guy, you old hodag." Tantra wrapped himself around No Mind.

Tenacity whispered to Big Man, "Tantra's three parts Yoga of the Body Heat."

When Tantra peeled away, No Mind was seen to have been licked clean. Scabs had formed on all the lesions. The muck was gone. He was warm and dry, down to his calves at least, where the stream was still slowly rising. "Thank you, all of you," No Mind said.

"Who are you, No Mind?" Big Man skewered him. "Tenacity and me both tagged you..."

"You didn't call it," Sorrow whined.

"...and all we saw was a hole. Who's in it?"

Ramrod straight, No Mind stared right back at Big Man. "All we are is a hole, Big Man, Tenacity—*sunyata*, buddha nature. Rightly seen, our true nature is emptiness."

It stopped him. That sort of talk always stopped Big Man. He looked away. It was something he knew he couldn't understand. Too much ego.

\#

NOT YOU! YOU'RE A CARRIER. STEP ASIDE, PLEASE.

\#

Big Man hadn't attained enlightenment. He hadn't seen through, and therefore he hadn't gotten through. No Mind, on the other hand, was the teacher of all the Econoline Vannies. *Zazen, zazen,*

zazen! Maybe the robes were right, maybe No Mind understood the thing that evaded Big Man: *sunyata*, emptiness. Angela must understand it too, damn her, just like Janus, the girl in the picture window, who could not, for all she might have wanted to, bore a little hole and pull him through. Big Man had taught her; now she was in the City, and he...

* * *

"You're next, Big Man. They're going to dyne me. I've passed! I'm through!"

"Wait! Let me kiss you. Let me touch you!"

"STEP ASIDE, PLEASE. OTHER PEOPLE ARE WAITING."

"You'll get through, Big Man. Just do zazen!"

* * *

"Bullshit," Tenacity shot back, "That hole ain't *sunyata*. That ain't buddha nature. That's a line of bull is what that is. Pick up your chin, Big Man, you dope. This guy is the hole we crawled out of. Somebody's running him. Somebody's reamed his brains and reupholstered."

No Mind was calm and clear. "It is buddha nature. When a thief looks at a wise man, he only sees the wise man's pocket."

"Yeah, well, I may be a thief, all right, but you're sure as hell no wise man."

The whaddayagets had been slowly, quietly encircling Tenacity and the two men. They sat in concentric rings, an acropolis of hodags. They were passing around strange powders and squeeze bottles full of boiling fluids, which they poured noisily into orifices fore and aft. Some commented on the action. Others groomed, scratched, dozed.

"Hey, Big Man!" No Mind paused and inclined his head like a translator waiting for the end of a phrase. "Where's your friend?

Where's Pirate?"

Big Man whirled around, fuming. "That bastard. Him and Angela. I knew it."

Chapter Eight

Pirate could tell them he had gone off to take a dump, or he could say he hadn't wanted to play tag—no matter what he said, Big Man wouldn't believe him. In truth, Pirate wanted to see what Angela did when she went off that way. Maybe there was something in it that would salvage his friendship with Big Man. Or maybe Big Man was right, and Pirate wanted to grab the wise, pretty girl with eyes like full moons, her head in his palms, her small shoulders inside the crook of his arms, and pull her lips against his lips.

Then again, maybe he was just curious, really curious, and there was nothing much else to give a damn about. Like it said on his belly, around the eight-spoked Wheel of the Dharma: "Party down!"

The slant passage was dry. Up ahead he saw green light feathering the edge stones of a turn in the oblique squeeze—Angela. He followed.

Pirate snaked between the slanting strata, moving gingerly where spar grazed his chest and arms. Up and down felt all wrong here, sandwiched between slanting sheets of rock. Sometimes a crystal—or Pirate's own nails, teeth, or sweaty calves—would catch a scintilla of light from an unknown source farther up the passage. The unguent would black out. Then only that glimmer and the feel of the rock told Pirate where he was going. He would pull ahead, and when the angle changed, or when the glimmer was eclipsed by his own body, the green glow would return—until the next time.

Eventually—minutes? hours?—the lower slab angled down, and the passage widened into a man-tall tube with a genuine, horizontal walking surface.

Just at the point where Pirate could stand on his feet again, he saw the first mural, lit faintly by diffused daylight from far above. There were little cream splotches on it: cumulus clouds. Schools of fish, rust-colored or iodine, swarmed above and below them. Cobalt-blue stick figures, vaguely human, were crossed by a tangle of scratches stained dark red.

A little farther down, there was a second mural. In its center Pirate saw a dark triangle of a man wearing a conical sorcerer's hat and a sequined robe, shoulders to toes. All in all, he was the shape of a volcano, and his beard flowed down like lava. His eyes were owls' eyes. He had the antlers of a stag, wolf ears, and the claws of a lion. The sorcerer stood above a Lilliputian skyline of buildings and towers, some half-hidden under the hem of his robe. In one upraised hand he held a *dorje*, a symbol of the City's power; with the other he was pushing a small package into the opening of a cave the size of his hand. There was an aura of yellow light around the opening and tiny people prostrating or kneeling reverently with clasped hands.

The next mural showed the cave that received the sorcerer's package. It was a perfect circle whose diameter was Pirate's height. The view was from inside the cave. From this perspective, the sorcerer's hand was gigantic, pushing the package in. In the foreground, a tiny man and woman with two small children were reaching out to receive the package. Their arms and hands, fingers spread wide, were like cilia sweeping in from the rim of the circle. The package, it could be seen here, was a woman swaddled like a baby. The swaddling might have been a winding cloth, but the woman was in foetal position, and her eyes were open, the face tinted pink and surrounded by a sunburst. Pirate began to feel that he recognized her.

He moved along the passage to the fourth mural, smaller than the rest, framed by twenty concentric squares. Each square was filled with crows in a tightly interlocking pattern, wing to beak, a plenum of crows. In the center square—domestic tranquility: the family seen in the previous mural, the tiny man and woman and their two children, were embracing and smiling. They all had halos limned with sulfate crystals. They stood on a dais in the center of a plaza teeming with people. Behind them was a semicircular backdrop of Gothic towers. Goddesses hovering overhead showered flower petals on them.

What could be the meaning of the owl-eyed hierophant of the City? Who were his angelic beneficiaries? And who was that swaddled woman, the hierophant's gift? Pirate leaned in to examine the tiny people—when the mural swung toward him. It was a hinged slab. An arm shot out and clutched Pirate's hair. Another hand grabbed his hip and yanked him up and in. The slab slammed shut.

Someone was spinning him and winding rags around his arms and legs as if they were dressing a corpse for burial. As they did so, his light diminished. He saw them by the light from the unguent on his face and neck, then his face only—cloth winding upward—then his forehead, and at last his eyes were covered as well. It could be delirium, but they had looked like the family in the murals: a man and a woman, both of them skeletal now and covered with gaping sores, and their two small children covered with silt.

A low rasp: "He must have got lost behind them others."

Then a child's voice: "He ain't with them others. He gots no clothes. He nekkid. He different. He don't smell like he come from no bone pit neither. And he ain't Jap'nese."

"They wasn't all Jap'nese. Not the female. And not the littl'un."

By the scratchy falsetto, Pirate thought this must be the woman: "He followin' Jello. He up to no good."

The child again: "Jello ours, ain't she? We brung her out."

"Hush. You know we ain't s'posta have nothin' to do with her no more."

The low rasp again: "All of yas shut up. Break's over. Them others'll be on the karst already. We'll do our rounds, then figger out what to do with him."

The woman: "Them others could be after Jello. We could warn her."

"Shut up, I said. Gassho now. We gonna do our *suchamis* and sit zen."

A bell rang. Four voices droned:

#

All beings one darkness, such am I.
All passions one doubt, such am I.
All gates the gate in, such am I.
Such is the great City, and such am I.

#

They said the whole thing three times, rang the bell twice more, and were silent. Nothing stirred for a long time. Terror lit Pirate's mind like a road flare. He strained to regulate his breathing within the tightly wound cloth. He tried to let his panic subside.

Once in a while, a child sniffed or fidgeted, and the father machine gunned, "No movin'."

Pirate twitched, and a bit of frayed cloth sagged down from one eye. He saw their faint green shadows. They were sitting cross-legged, facing the far wall of their tiny pit. They lived there like shit in a diverticulum, their own miniscule Dharma Cave. Why?

The tall, hairy one turned his head. "Fuck damn. Light leak. Keep sittin'." He stood. Pirate, paralyzed, was leaning against a pit wall like a tipsy amphora. He watched the father's figure loom larger till his face filled Pirate's entire field of vision. The father's eyes were like dried and shriveled milkweed pods. He snarled, squinting as he scratched into the threads around Pirate's eye. "You so much as wrinkle and I'll whup you. It gots to be dark, mind? We sittin' zen here. We savin' all beings. We gettin' our asses into the City, like what we was promised. You sit still." The fabric shifted, and Pirate was blind again.

"The City owes us for Jello, don't it, Daddy?"

"No talkin'. No movin'."

He could wiggle the fingers of his left hand, Pirate discovered. What if he poked through? What if his light shone out again?

The bell rang, a pure high sound, and they began chanting:

#

All hail the miraculous picture wall!
All hail its holy instructions!
We are the chosen foetus bearers and stuff like that.
Hail the birth canal of the womb of the City!
Hail the great spirit of the City and other stuff,
What entered our dreams and called us into the earth,
To deliver his only-begotten somethin' to the Saha World.
All Hail The Gimlet of True Cityzen Practice!
And some other stuff like that.
SVAHA!

#

"Isn't it s'posta be 'some other *things* like that?'"—one of the children.

The mother's voice: "Shush. Sometimes we say it one way, and sometimes another, mind?"

Pirate was pummeled by rough hands that felt him up and down through the ratty cloth. "We can't kill him. If we killed him, it'd be lousy karma. It'd slow us down sure. 'Course if he suffocate in them rags, it ain't our fault."

"Throw him back, Hon'."

"Don't be stoopit. We let them eight, nine, ten get by stinkin' of bones the way they did. That was wrong. We was slow. City'll know. I feel it."

"I feel it too, Daddy."

"Me too, Daddy."

"City'll know. It'll be angry, won't it? Jello down here again.

Them eight, nine, ten bums maybe wanna jump her. I don't like it. At least this number eleven or what ain't gonna hurt no Incarnation."

"City gonna make us sit longer before we get in, Daddy?"

"Clam up, youse kids. Kin I git a word in edgewise? ...Shit." Someone grabbed Pirate's thumb where he had forced it through the fabric. "Gah! Damn! How you s'posta concentrate your mind? Lookit that shit. He won't keep the damn light in."

Pirate felt a sharp blow to his hand. He keeled over onto his stomach. *Good. They're not going to kill me. As long as I can keep things happening, it's good. As long as I can mix it up.* He found that he could move his jaw. He stuck his tongue out and started licking the fabric. It became wet and sagged in slightly. He sucked. Then he could gnaw on it and work open the hole with his tongue and lips.

"Damn! He lightin' up the damn floor. Don't you got no consideration? We on a path here. We doin' zazen. Damn!"

"Toss him out, Hon'. It's time for next round now. We gots to sit."

"You think so?"

"We wound him good. He gonna die before he be free. Not our fault, either. No bad karma. We gonna git back our tape when he dead—don't worry about that."

"Hmm!"—the father. Pirate snaked another few fingers out through the cloth. "Gah!" Then he heard the slab push out again. Eight hands pressed into his flank and rolled him toward the opening. He fell hard, then heard the wall close again just before the real pain hit.

* * *

They were wrong about Pirate. He wrenched at his winding cloth. He chewed and ripped. A patch between his feet had shredded against the cave wall; he pushed his legs apart and tore it open.

His whole body ached. The pain in his head came in pulses like hammer strikes on an anvil, and nearly as bad was the instinctive flinching in-between, when he could feel the next beat coming. He burst the cloth as if he could break the pain that way. He pushed against it, and it gave in half a dozen places. One rip for the father, one rip for his wife, two rips for the bedeviled children—maybe Pirate could pry open that slab and tattoo "PARTY DOWN!" on their faces with his nails.

"You poor baby."

"Angela?" She was there and she wasn't there. She faded in and out like the image of the moon in a bay window, when a night wind swings it open and sucks it back, clacking and rattling.

"You poor baby."

Pirate swept his hand through her pelvis. Nothing stopped it. "I must have really whacked my head."

"My swaddling clothes!" She leaned over the brown, rotted tatters trailing from Pirate's ankles. "They kept them all these years. Did they hurt you bad?"

"Bad enough to be see things, I guess."

"You ain't seein' things, Pirate. I'm up ahead, listenin' to the City. It happens to me like this. Don't be scared."

"I'm not scared. I'm crazy."

"I get powers when I listen to the City. I go lotsa places at once, like a transcat almost. Don't ask me what I am, Pirate—I dunno... Wait a minute." The image—light without substance—waved and trembled like a reflection rippling in a pool. "Yes..." She wasn't speaking to Pirate. "...Yes, I hear you. All right, I'll take him." She paused a moment, then began to sob. "Oh, do I have to die? Do I really have to? Can't I ever have him back? I know that. I know. I will. Of course I will. But I'm so unhappy. I'm real unhappy now."

"Angela, who are you talking to?"

"I don't know. The City. You know I came from there, don'tcha, Pirate? Ain't that why you snuck after me?"

"Is it you in the murals?"

"It must be. I think they painted 'em there to show the Catchers what they was s'posta do. First they got 'em down here with dreams. They couldn't rig 'em up with no crystal sets. They're too stupid. They used dreams, even though it's not as good. Then them pictures. Now the Catchers just go on like before, poor things, in the dark, underground. They're too dumb too leave."

"Jesus fuck damn! I'm a lunatic. Angela honey, I just want to crack a few Circenses and boil couch-grass seeds. I think I got it down now. I think if I grease 'em up and stir fry 'em after, then they'll be okay. Flavor 'em kind of nutty, you know? Ow, my head! I never gave a toot about the damn City, either, so how come I'm sitting up God's asshole talking to a wind egg?"

"You used to sit, Pirate."

"I never did."

"You used to sit day and night, like the Catchers practically. I know. You had enough *joriki* to light Interstate 90 to the Illinois border."

"Don't give me that."

"Then you made Suds and them guys cut words onto your belly and pour ink in 'em."

"That's right—*PARTY DOWN!*"

"And you stopped sittin' zen. How come, Pirate? What did you see?"

"I got tired of it, that's all. Period. Full stop. End of story. Tired of it. Who's asking me, anyway? Is it you, Angela, or is it whoever's using you?"

"I dunno. I dunno." Like a double image coming into focus, Angela walked into her own body. Pirate touched her hand, a real hand. "Go back, Pirate."

"That bastard doesn't deserve you."

"Big Man's your friend. You come here for him, 'cause you love him, Pirate. I love him too."

"I know you do, Angela. But you should stop."

"I can't. Some people been through hell and back for a lover. Me, I been through heaven and back, Pirate, and it's worse."

The waves of pain were dwindling. Pirate straightened himself and took Angela's other hand. He moved toward her until he felt her nipples graze his chest. He said, "This is the City."

"Yes," she said, and they were making love. He had not intended it—he had figured that she would push him away; in fact, he had been relying on it. His black curls fell like a cataract between their cheeks. Her hands found his shoulder blades, she pulled him to her, and then she leaned against him and danced him back against a sheer wall. She held tight and scissored him with her legs and took him inside her. Now Pirate was a passenger on a ghost train, barred down, buckled in, nothing to do but undulate and feel. She wept as they swelled and exploded into each other. When they were done, she moved away and gradually made herself stop weeping.

"Go back. The whaddayas got a way of fixing you. You're all cut up. I'll be back in a jiffy."

"Wait a minute. What...?"

"Go, Pirate. Go now. I'll be there in a jiffy. Pirate, don't be mad at me. It won't be long before you understand everything."

"Mad at you? Why did we do that? Tell me what you were talking about with the City."

"Don't be mad, Pirate. Tell No Mind I said he could come."

"Are you crazy? He hates us. Bastard'll kill us first chance he gets."

"He's s'posta come—go now, Pirate, please."

"Did we just make love because the City wants you to?"

"Go. I'm beggin' you, Pirate."

Pirate swung round and made his way back to the oblique squeeze.

Chapter Eight

***

On the broken highway under a moonless sky in a black year past, they're so drunk that their limbs feel like liquid. Pirate keeps grabbing and squeezing things or knocking his head into them, just to feel solid. Everything is spinning. For a while, they amuse themselves by jumping from car-top to car-top all along 90 from the On Ramp to the Rest Stop. There they collapse, clothes and skin covered with rust, laughing and shouting ancient obscenities. All through the Jam, windows roll up.

"Do it, Suds."

"No. Hell. You don't want me to do that, Pirate, man. Your belly is a fuck damn work of art. Looka dem spokes, huh? Eight spokes, like the Eightfold Fuck Damn Noble Path."

"Write it, you icchantika meat sucker."

Virya lowers herself halfway onto Pirate, then falls the rest of the way. "No. You're gonna get in before any of us, Pirate... Amitabha, I think I'm gonna be sick... You don't wanna do this."

"Don't tell me nothing." He can't locate Virya well enough to push her off him. "I understand everything. I've seen it now, man. I'm complete. I've got kensho. I could whiz by Control tomorrow."

"Well, why the fuckeroo don't you?" — Virya's mouth on his nose.

"'Cause I seen what I am, man. I understand everything."

Suds shoves Virya aside and stares at Pirate unsteadily while Pirate blubbers. Suds asks: "What do you understand, man? What have you seen?"

"I'm part of a transcat, man. I saw it. I was in deep, samadhi below samadhi, right to the Tushita Heaven, man. And I could see clear past the whole world to where everything ties together. I saw the bottoms of all the things my life is just the tops of. This brain" — clawing at his head — "these eyes, they don't belong to me. Something else is running me, man. I don't want to look any more." By sheer luck, he manages to grab Suds's arm and pull him into his own face. "Do it. 'Party down!'"

Suddenly cold sober — "You got a knife?"

Chapter Nine

No Mind caught Big Man's eye and held it. "Is there something between Pirate and Angela?"

"Back off, will you?"

"You don't know who your friends are, Big Man."

No Mind could see the wheels turning. Big Man's lower lip trembled, like a child's before crying. His hands clenched and unclenched. "Maybe you're right," Big Man said.

Enough for now, No Mind's Voice told him. *You do well, Noble One. You must divide friend from friend and join them to you. It is an upaya, a skillful means for the enlightenment of all beings. Remember the City. Remember...*

"Divide what from who?" A bird like a bicycle horn flattened its round, rubbery proboscis against No Mind's chest. No Mind instinctively swiped it away.

"Hey, killer," Tenacity warned, "mind my hodags. You don't touch a whimsy or a feather spine, hear, or we'll eat you up."

"The thing bumped him, Tenacity," Big Man said.

"You ain't really jealous, you big fart, that's the thing that gets me. But I can't see what it's covering up." Tenacity puffed out his little cheeks and squinted, then slapped the air out.

The bicycle-horn bird was hovering for another pry at No Mind's thoughts, when there was a sudden disturbance. Every creature hushed. They leaned. They listened. Just as suddenly, they whooped and funneled, screaming, into their hole. Only Tenacity and one ancient whaddaya remained in the junction room with Big Man and No Mind.

Tenacity scowled and shook his head. "Transcat."

"Here?" Big Man asked him.

"Here. So what, that's what I say. But they give most of us cave hoots the willies. Just sit tight. It'll pass."

"I don't feel a thing," Big Man said.

"I do," No Mind said. "It's like tentacles."

"It's not. Shut up." Tenacity sat on his lower rim and squeezed as if to take a dump. His face reddened. "Come close and dry off. You skins die quick if you stay cold." No Mind and Big Man came near. Tenacity was radiating heat. His green glow became a shade lighter. The men warmed their hands and turned round to dry their backsides.

"Where is it, Tenacity?" Big Man asked him.

But one of the others answered, "She's all over you." The old whaddayaget was all wrinkles, and nothing wrinkling. "She's in you and out of you like cosmic rays. She's using your body like a swinging door. I'd be all pins and needles if it were me. Are you feeling kind of... nostalgic?"

Big Man tilted his head sideways and looked at the ceiling. "There was this woman. We used to sit together. Not Angela. No, I mean, a while ago. Lord, she lived in one of the last real houses up over Route 90..."

"That's the transcat's belly, that mood of yours. Not the whole thing. Part of it. I see some of the rest of it twitching through a black void on the cold side of Pluto, five or six years from now." The wrinkles shifted, bunched, and reshuffled into a tent-like configuration. "Don't distress yourself. It'll pass. It's not you."

Tenacity was cooling down. "Old wrinkly feels everything all over the universe practically. We call him, 'Scope. Wanna guess what he's made of?"

No Mind flicked some dried mud off Big Man's shoulder. "Who was she, Big Man?"

"Come on, guess, Big Man." Tenacity pushed No Man aside.

Big Man shook off the cobwebs and looked straight at 'Scope. "Melancholy. Clarity. Detachment. Information. Elasticity. Beeohtees. I don't know the proportions. And a little girl in there, something like a little girl—was that a mistake when they statted you?"

"Hoo! That's my skinbag. Don't he have the eye." Tenacity

kissed Big Man on the lips and backfired. An anxious murmur rose from the whaddayagets' pit. "Pipe down, you yellows—it was me."

'Scope started pulsing out words, deep and clear. His wrinkles undulated like oscilloscope lines. "It was a mistake. I was a trial run. There's a number like me they use in the City, only without the little girl bred in. Mind you, it's only the sugar and spice parts I got—no Miss Prissy, no Miss Bossy—so there."

Tenacity rolled onto his side. "Tell these lubbers all about it, 'Scope. We got nothing to do till the transcat's gone."

"I was gonna. They made me early on, but that's not how come I'm old. I was born old. They had to do me that way. It was just after the Mercury Anomaly, the second one, the big one, when the transcategoricals shimmered in, and Descartes and Newton and Einstein and Hume and everybody in the whole history of Western Civilization who ever mentioned a point or a line or a frame of reference or a sequence of one thing after another—they were all quite suddenly vestigial... I bet you wish you knew half of what I do."

'Scope covered his "mouth" as if he had hiccoughed, and then went on. "Everybody Earthside had always thought the world was built up out of particles of one kind or another—sensations or quarks or souls. Well, now they saw that that idea was upside-down: the world is built down from one big, undifferentiated whole, down into particles. And the particles are provisional. The borders between things are unreal, like pocks on a putty ball: squoosh! and they're all rearranged. Nobody had ever thought that big since the Upanishads or the Mahayana Sutras. That's where Buddhism started to come into favor.

"But who were these transcats? You know what I mean? That's what people were saying. How can we get rid of them? That's what everybody wanted, right off, as if that was ever an option. It would be like trying to gnaw off your brains and heart. We're laced through with transcats like brine with salt. I was supposed to be a kind of search-and-destroy machine, but all I want to do is dress up Betsy McCall."

"It's gone now, isn't it?" No Mind said.

"No." Old 'Scope pursed his wrinkles to wet them. "Sit tight—that's the best thing. This one's just passing through. It won't be long.

"It's ironic when you think about it. The tech they used to make me, the skinbags got it all from transcats—from watching them, and from being watched by them, the funny way that works. As if water could taste you because you swallow it. They had to rewrite all the science books and stop thinking of skins as skins. Mind you, they'd always known they were permeable to air and moisture and thoughts and feelings, but people wanted to hold onto the idea that everybody was something apart. The transcats made that hard.

"The Planners made me to scan the universe for transcats, to log every border between one thing and another, every way you could define it, cross-referencing each phenomenon for fifteen-billion light years in every direction. I was supposed to be a sieve. They were going to use me to pan the universe for transcats. They figured that then they could get rid of them somehow, or at least get out of their way... It's leaving now... but, you know, you can't.

"The Planners focused down their big n-dimensional hypostat guns on fragments of twenty or thirty cosmology mavens and astrographers, along with a tightrope walker I believe, for his particular concentration. They also hypostatted a number of ephemerides, yes, a bunch of technical beeohtees, and a part of Tycho Brahe, which they picked up in the dyne pool where the transcats like to feed.

"But they didn't have their tech down, did they, all that non-dual transcat-think being so new to them? Any hypostat beam cuts back and forth through time and zigzags through space like a spastic's backstitch. Some little girl in what's left of Kenya, a seven year old snoozing, spooned against her mama's belly in their cool thatch hut, was smack in the path of the hypostatic ray. And pow zingo! When you hear that nya-nya-nya nya-nya in my voice, why, it's her.

"You can all relax now. The thing is gone."

"It didn't work then?" Big Man said.

"Naw. It was all wrong from jump. The transcats are in this soup so tight, the second you try to scan them, you hit a self-reference jam. They're a part of your scanner, turns out, or your eye, or your discursive thinking. All you get is the little glimpses like what we just had here—a shimmy and a fast exit. Like quanta, you can never get the whole picture, because the measurement changes the data. I want my mommy."

Tenacity's tinny baby laugh stopped them. "Should we sound the all-clear?"

'Scope shook rock dust off his lower waves. "Wait. I got a beeohtee in me. Listen up." 'Scope flexed himself into a perfect rectangle with narrow, horizontal stripes. In a moment, the stripes started pulsing, and the pulses were accompanied by sound:

* * *

ON THE LESSONS OF THE TRANSCATEGORICALS
(Being Chair Elect Wexler's Installation Address
to City Planning,
In Plenary Session, November 30, 04 Post Transcat)

When the Second Orbital Anomaly was first discovered—some of you were still children then—the bankruptcy of the hard sciences had already become apparent to our leading minds. Physical studies had dead-ended in their own originating principles. The speed of light confined exploration and expansion to our immediate intragalactic neighborhood. Heisenberg's relationship, the impossibility of deter-

mining subatomic events independently of an infecting observer, limited our manipulation of microcosmic phenomena. One saw increasingly detailed studies of decreasingly significant subjects, filling in the blanks of work done decades before. We could reach the outer planets, but could do little. We produced food we could not distribute. We perfected engines, and ran out of fuel. And meanwhile, world population was at the bursting point.

Then came the new Mercury Anomaly. The path of a planet in space-time, we found to our dismay, could be an appendage of a creature whose body extended across galaxies, with holes many parsecs in diameter and gaps millennia in duration. The transcategoricals, as is now common knowledge, could combine a phrase of music, a particular human jawbone, a black hole, all the entities of a certain mass or shape in the universe, and so on, in a single intelligent being, with whom communication began to be possible.

The Newtonian concept of point mass was unseated. Cartesian analyses of space and time, however extravagant and non-Euclidean, became passé. Impenetrability of matter, conservation and symmetry laws of all stripes were superseded. The experimental method itself— repeatability, parsimony, falsifiability, the null hypothesis—instant atavisms.

We were like primitives whose coconut currency became suddenly worthless alongside the explorers' dubloons. There were suicides in those days. Is there a person here now who has not been touched by one? People discovered they were part of a transcat and lost the will to go on.

Who understood this first? The scientists? No. It was the mystics, and in particular the Buddhist mystics, whose codified insights had prefigured and inspired cosmologists and quantum physicists even before the Anomaly. It was natural then that the language and culture of our Western civilization should have become permeated with Buddhist language and ideology—the ideology of non-dual logic, of non-substantiality, of unlimited spacio-temporal extent in which humanity was one small, basically vacuous element. The fertilization of science by Buddhism, catalyzed by the contact with transcats, led to the technologies of Cityfication: hypostasis and hypodynamics.

It is now generally conceded that the initial attempts to apply transcat science to the population question were deficient in fundamental ways. Interpenetrating space-time has been at best a partial solution. No one would submit to suburban life today unless he or she had already been placed there. Mutual occupation of space-time, somatic overlapping and the like, are ineffective without ego-loss.

Only look at the suburbs. The same frictions eventuate, the same centripetal forces of psychology that have always created tensions, crime, war, and mass suffering. No one doubts this today. We have gone past that. Mere stacking, however dense, will never serve. With the risk of sounding trite, I say again, that 'to enter the City, you have to get rid of the idea of self-gain.'

FROM THE FLOOR: What about love? This is relevant. When you love somebody, their gain is yours, but you haven't lost your own self. And what about Doubt Mass? Without Doubt Mass, won't a City stagnate?

Kindly refrain from interrupting, madam, or I shall be compelled to ask the bailiff to escort you to the door. We are conducting this meeting in conventional 3-space to make it accessible to the general public; however, we shall compact, or dyne and stat, to finish our business, if we see privileges being abused. As to love, however, Doubt Mass, and the rest, they are well and good for the unenlightened, but the true Cityzen sees them to be vacuous. There is no room for such egoistic phenomena in our City.

* * *

"I think I was at that meeting." Big Man squinted to remember. "That was a long time ago, though." He shook his head. "I hate torching my brains over gone shit."

Tenacity, who had been watching Big Man's reaction with great interest, looked disappointed. "Yeah, just like you're supposed to," he mumbled.

"What's up, Tenacity?" No Mind asked him.

"It so happens the ideer of love wasn't completely left out, back at the beginning of the City. They shooed it out later on— love, passion, Doubt Mass, all that juice. I got a sort of brother who's the turnstile at Control—he knows City business, butt and smacker. They statted all them berzerker scats into one skinbag and hooted him into the hicks."

No Mind was troubled. His mind became opaque. His Voice pounded on smoked, doubled glass; he didn't hear. "So he's out here somewhere, this hypostat? In the world?"

"Yeah, in the world, in the Saha World," drawled Tenacity.

"Whoever that is must be desperate to get in, to be whole again," No Mind said. "Whoever that is must have Doubt Mass like a mountain."

Big Man said, "Is it you, No Mind?"

"No"—suddenly weary, defeated—"it isn't me."

The whaddayagets were clambering out of their hole. The smoked, doubled glass shattered. No Mind's eyes cleared, and he did what he was asked to. He slapped Big Man on the back, winked, and pointed to the oblique opening. "I smell something funky coming out of there. I think you should be the one to help Pirate out, Big Man."

Chapter Ten

I saw rock dust spitting out of the oblique, and I knew it was Pirate grinding through. Angela wouldn't leave a trace. I walked to the opening and stuck my head in. I could see the top of his head worming toward me like a baby—or a shit.

No Mind whispered, "I'd have a hard time keeping the precepts right now, if I were you."

"You're not him, killer, and you already broke a couple." Tenacity jetted into No Mind's ankles, tripping him. "Relax, Big Man. Bend, don't break, okay?"

Pirate didn't see me until his forehead touched my nose. He craned his head up, and I smiled in his face. "What's that smell on you, Pirate? Is that Angela?"

"Let me out, Big Man. It's not like that."

"You missed our game. Afraid of being tagged?"

Tenacity whined, "I'm tagging him, Big Butt—he's nine parts true, and the tenth has nothing to do with Jello."

"I'm sorry to say, I don't see it that way." No Mind flinched as if he were expecting Tenacity to charge him, but the little bugger stayed put.

"Here. Let me help you out, bro." I grabbed under Pirate's armpits and yanked. He yelled bloody murder. The spar was shredding his skin like a fruit peeler. As soon as most of his arms were out, he shoved me back and scrambled to his feet. He wasn't hurt bad. He was scratched up. Some whaddayas came by to heal him, but he shooed them away.

"Hey! Hey!" We heard Angela's voice echoing back up the oblique. "You dopes, you're fighting, ain'tchas?"

Pirate and I stung each other's eyes dead on, like lizards set to spring. His ugly mouth twitched with the rest of him, just aching to swipe me.

"Come on, Pirate, take your best shot." Arms at my sides,

palms forward, I walked into his face. "You took my woman. Take me."

No Mind and the whaddayagets were jabbering at me from behind—just jazz to me; I was juiced for Pirate. He was a butcher's chart, as far as I was concerned. I just stood there, choosing my cuts.

He breathed out a long one, looked down and then looked up again, soulfully. "Big Man..."

I laid my fingers on his chest and pushed.

He came at me, winding up for his pathetic roundhouse right, and I was ready for it. I had his breadbasket all picked out for my knee to land in. But he never came through with the right. His shoulder pulled forward—a sucker's lead—and jerked to a stop.

Angela was holding his fist. "You dumb assholes, knock it off. You're not s'posta be doin' that now. Darn shoo, Big Man, I thought you wanted to be a Cityzen. Where'd all your samadhi go, Big Man? Don't you know Pirate's one of them sentient beings you're s'posta be savin', just like you're one of his?" She slid her other leg out of the oblique passage.

"That's right," I said. "Don't let me mess up your pretty boy. Lecture me, Angela. You been to the City and back, haven't you? You know it all." Pirate bit his tongue.

"Stop it. Lookit, the stream's come up into the junction. We gotta move on. No Mind, did Pirate tell you I said you could come?"

"No."

Angela shot Pirate an angry look. Pirate tried to say something, then gave up; he just rolled his eyes and turned away. She said, "Well, No Mind, you can. Just stay close, 'cause I got no more glow stuff for you. There are some places up ahead where you could fall way down and spill your brains in the dark.

"Through the keyhole now. Straight ahead. We don't take no turnoffs till we hit a big shaft. It's a long drop, then there's a slow incline up to the karst. Let's go. It was good to see you, Tenacity.

I love all you hodags—you know that. We just gotta go."

Tenacity stood on the point of his tail. He let the tail fold under him like a column of z's, then spring out again. He bounced onto my shoulder. If he hadn't retrofired with exhaust, I would have collapsed under the impact—I was that surprised.

"I'm coming along. I like this asshole," he said.

Angela's eyes melted. For a second I thought she would say, "Me, too." Then a shadow passed over them. Her face hardened. "Suit yourself," is what she said. For me, what a relief.

'Scope and the old orangutan were already squabbling over who was going to be the big boss in Tenacity's absence. I prodded Tenacity off my shoulder, then ducked into the keyhole—"Let me scout ahead"—hoping Pirate would get the point.

And he did. He charged in right after. "Wait up, Big Man. I'll help."

"Hey!" Angela started after us.

"Hey!" Tenacity joined her. "You dumb one-notes. You gonna kill each other now? Jeez, I'd like to meet the asshole who created Man. I'd give him a piece of my mind—the *Veltschmerz* probably. Wait up."

I sprinted down the passage. Pirate followed me close. I heard him stumble and fall a few times, but I knew he'd keep after me. He was already banged up bad, but I knew him for a bulldog. I'd relied on that in more than a couple tight places.

When I reached the shaft, I wasn't tired at all. Angela could have spared No Mind the lecture—the unguent was no good here anyway. A shimmer of reflected light coming up from the shaft immediately blacked out the unguent.

I got down on my belly and peeked into the abyss. It looked to be maybe eighty, a hundred feet down. It ran fairly wide at first, with good cracks to jam a fist in for climbing down. For the bottom half, it looked too smooth for good purchase but narrow enough, barely, to ratchet down, spread-eagled against the circumference. You'd need to face the bottom—not a comfortable prospect. Angela must have some trick for this chimney, but I wasn't going to wait for her. It looked to me like a damned good spot to flush out the bastard Pirate.

So I started on down. The smoothness of the flowstone in that passage was fine for echoes. I could hear Angela's voice — "Hey! Hey! Hey, Pirate! Hey, Big Man! Knock it off, you galoots. (*Galoots! Galoots! Galoots!*) Wait for me! (*Me! Me! Me! Me!*)" I chinned down and pushed my fist hard into a bucket-shaped pit just below the lip of the hole. I lowered myself in. From there I was able to slide a little and stem over to a long crack. I could hand-over-hand it for thirty feet before the crack pinched out. Then it was a new ball game.

I wanted to have my tête-à-tête with Pirate down below, in the whale's throat. There was poetry to it. We'd both be pressing hands and feet against the circumference for dear life. I figured I could hold on a lot longer, and then his meat would be mine. Or else he'd just lose hold and die all on his own. And I could watch.

The rock was dead vertical and cold. I climbed down as quickly as I could, without forgetting what a body looks like after smashing down a hundred feet, caroming off walls and slamming to bed on dumb rock. I made sure I always had three holds, hands and feet, with only one limb at a time in space.

I was well down the crack when Pirate peeked in. I leaned out from my hold and looked up. I saw him, black and white in the dark above me swimming with sky flowers and paisleys.

"This is stupid, Big Man. You're crazy, you know that? I don't know what I'm doing here. I don't want to hurt you."

"You think you could?"

"Shit."

Hugging the rock, he lowered himself down. He tickled his feet along the waves of rock face, looking for a hold. He moved just like a fat man easing into hot bath water. He found the seam, stacked his fingers in, wedged his foot below, and torqued on down.

I was down to a pinky lock near the bottom of the crack. It was time to vault off and slap all fours against the circumference of the hole, spread-eagle in the whale's throat like a stuck fishbone, when I had an evil inspiration—I sprang out facing up instead of down. "Hey, Pirate!" There was a split-second of limbo, the dead point, midair, as I heaved out. Then I was in there, tensioned between the walls, looking up at Pirate as if I were relaxing on a hammock. "Take me, man. I'm yours."

Pirate stopped to look down, and I thought he would vomit. He nearly lost his hold. "Shit." He labored down the seam, fist over clumsy fist. When he was a few feet above me, he paused, sucked his chest into the rock, and, one by one, shook the blood back into his arms. He scanned the shaft for a good hold, and realized there wasn't any. Then he understood why I had wedged that way, that it wasn't only to taunt him. He took a deep breath, groaned it out, and Geronimoed across the hole.

It looked like he would take us both down. He was out of control. It was completely up to the forces of Nature—gravity vs. the inertia of his wild, first spring. In that crazy second, I had to remind myself that to flinch was to fall; I had to keep pressing out. Then his hands and one foot slapped the rock, slipped a tad, and frictioned to a stop.

Pirate was looking down at me, his head at about my one o'clock. He was twitching all over and panting. Whenever he moved his head his black curls would brush against my cheek or shoulder. His sweat rained on me. "I just want to talk to you, Big Man."

If I laughed, I would die. I wouldn't get to enter the City. I wouldn't get to straighten out Pirate. "Talk."

"I can't stay like this till the crows come, Big Man."

"Talk fast."

Angela and Tenacity had reached the chute. I saw their dim shadows edge into view on either side of Pirate's head. "Open your eye, Beefsteak," Tenacity yelled.

Angela whimpered, "Avalokita, dear, sweet Lord Avalokita, don't let them get hurt down there."

"Let's get down to it, Big Man. What's really eating you?"

"You know what's eating me."

"I know what it's not. I know it's not me and Angela. You push her away every time she comes close. Why, Big Man? Why?"

Tenacity yelled down, "Come on, you oaf. Where's that zazen of yours? You can't see when you're pumping hate. Open your eye and tag the man. He's leveling with you."

"Shut up, up there." I was getting confused. "She doesn't want me. She says she wants me, but she disappears. She's playing me for a sucker. We plan together. We make love together. We sit together. I teach her how, damn it. Then she gets into the City, and I'm still here, on the dark side, on the dumb side, on the hick side, all alone, cracking Circenses and getting turned back. '*Not you. Too much ego. Step aside.*'"

"Who the hell are you talking about? Not Angela. She's not in the City. She's right here, Big Man. When you went to Control, she stayed behind to wait for you. What are you talking about? Who do you mean, Big Man? You don't mean...?"

"Janus."

It was quiet down there. All I could hear was our breath, mine and Pirate's, and the slow trickle of water seeping over the rim. My mind was quiet, too—for the first time since Janus had been hypodyned into the City. Now I saw it—her ghost infested every part of me, everything I said and did. For a moment, one knot of pain at the center of my mind sucked away all the petty beefs, and my heart cleared. Janus.

* * *

...Remember: I stood there that day, holding up the line. The guards prodded me with their karuna rods. I hardly felt them. Janus was going,

the picture-window girl. "Zazen, Big Man. Zazen. You can do it too. Zazen." After all, it's what we had always wanted, wasn't it? And then the "sardine" shuttle, the On Ramp, the long walk up Route 90, alone, to her father's house, and the rock through that big picture window. I hadn't known glass shattered that way, falling straight down, all at once, like a sheet of water. I had thought it would explode somehow, dramatically, and not just fall...

* * *

"*Amitabha,* it's still risin'. It's flowin' up through the keyhole" — Angela, far above.

"Janus is a Cityzen, a saint," I said.

"Yes, she made it through, and you didn't."

"Yes."

"Big Man, Angela's not Janus."

It wasn't a safe thing to do, but I began to cry. A thin stream of water was washing down the sides of the chute, lessening the friction that held us fifty feet above a hard landing. And somebody was inching down toward us. It wasn't Angela or Tenacity — I could hear them bellow from the top of the shaft, but I couldn't make out what they were saying.

Then I saw No Mind's face at my eleven o'clock. I stopped crying. Pirate's fist shot out at me. I dodged and nearly lost my hold. No Mind's arm wrapped around Pirate's face. "Move down. Move down. I've got him, Big Man. He won't hurt you now."

Chapter Eleven

On the karst the monks found a crack where a lost river surfaced. They tarried there to wash off the grue and stink of the bone pit they had climbed through. "It's the fastest way to the karst," Bobo Shin had told them. "Anyone who shudders is no zen man."

Rinzai had a headache.

"I'll massage you. I'm good." Mukan's hands slid down like cool water over Rinzai's small, shaven head.

It soothed him. His eyes closed. He sighed. There was plenty of sun here, inside the ring of mountains. The sun warmed him. It dried him. It never rained here. All the rain was milked from the clouds when they were blown up the outsides of the mountains. That's why the City Planners had moved them there, hypodyned the entire area from parts of Afghanistan and Yugoslavia, changed them into transcat jazz and statted them down again a few miles off Route 90. Ahh...

Then the Voice in his head thundered again, and he had to squeeze his mind shut with all the muscles in his head and neck, to make it stop. No Mind's crystal set had lashed a sore in Rinzai, like the sore that trainers lash in circus animals, then merely touch to make them obey.

"All phenomena are transient." Mukan dug his fingers into the knots. "Relax, little man... Why have you stayed on with us?"

"Where would I go? Angela is gone."

"Your mother?"

Rinzai tensed so hard, he felt like a fireball from the shoulders up, and from there down—nothing. It worked a little. It muted the echoes in his head. "*Your mother?*" The words cut in, plied nerve from nerve, muscle from rigid muscle, and in the fissures, tears welled. "*Your mother?*" The Voice planned to kill her. Bobo Shin wanted it too, and Clara. "*Your mother?*" Why not? He remembered no other. Only sleep. Sleep was his mother, on an empty belly in a safe place, a ditch maybe, off Interstate 90, or under a rusted chassis on the ridgepole of some gerrymandered ghost town. Sleep held him and rocked him, stroked his hair and lullabied—or was that his own hand, his own voice fading into drowsiness, into the warm salt sea of sleep? *"Your mother?"*

"Yes."

"Ah!" Mukan shook his head sadly. Only a little older than Rinzai, he kissed the boy's head and delicately removed his hands. It was useless. "Ah! Bobo Shin Roshi is my dad. It doesn't matter. He treats me like any monk. It is the spiritual lineage that counts, not the biological."

Then Rinzai had to close again, his ears, his muscles, his thoughts. He had said exactly what he always wanted to say— *Yes, Angela is my mother.* The tears streamed out of him like water from Moses's rock. But with their soft flow came the Voice again. *"Kill Angela. Kill her. She is icchantika. Kill."*

Bobo Shin strutted by, shot Rinzai and Mukan a suspicious glance, and walked on. He fiddled conspicuously with his earphone. After he had passed them, he said without turning back or slowing down, "Mukan! Rinzai! Get up. Stand up. No sitting down."

* * *

Bobo Shin reviewed his troops. The monks threw one another onto the ground, practicing holds, breaking holds, flipping, punching, growling. They were not very good at it. The bindings on their voluminous sleeves often gave way; the cloth trailed out, tripping some, blinding others, getting in people's mouths.

The monks seemed hopeless until Bobo Shin directed them to use their gimlets. Each monk had one of the sharp, little knives in his sleeve. If anything, they were more awkward now, more inept-looking, because more hideously overcautious. But

Bobo Shin saw that none of that mattered a damn. They didn't have to be great fighters. There were a good number of them, and they were armed.

"You stink of the bone pit," Bobo Shin thundered. "We have climbed down through hell. We have rolled in skulls still half-packed with meat. We have climbed down through viscera and gore. We have smelled the eight kinds of death and the forty-two sorts of dissolution and decay of the human body. You are blood-drinking, hell-breathing demons. Pay attention, you devils. Nothing can stop you.

"The precepts of the realized zens tell us to refrain from killing sentient beings. Now you devils must perfect a deeper understanding of this precept. Sometimes, to kill is to refrain from killing. Killing the dharma is real killing. Killing human beings is illusory. What is there to die? *Sunyata*—nothing. You are all demons. You are all invincible gods."

The monks roared and brandished their gimlets. Some were actually cut, and Bobo Shin had to restrain their assailants. When Clara emerged from a small, natural basin in which she had been relieving herself, Bobo Shin confessed to her, "I hate this. I don't mean a word of it. They are all idiots. You can't get good zen students these days. You can't hit them hard enough to make them understand."

"Why don't you give them bigger weapons?"

"It would frighten them too much. They would run away from me."

"Are you trying to get them to do this?" Clara planted her feet at shoulder's width. She placed her hands on her hips, bent her knees slightly to find a firm center, and exhaled with a slow hiss that Rinzai could hear from twenty yards away. In one brisk movement, lizard-like, her hand arrowed high, holding the gimlet. Bobo Shin, startled, looked up at it.

Clara undulated slowly. She lowered the gimlet, then threw it from hand to hand. Rinzai did not see her throw it. He only saw the gimlet appear first in one hand, then in the other.

Suddenly, she whirled. The gimlet flashed out. Her fist pressed against Bobo Shin's heart. He shrieked involuntarily. He sank to his knees. Clara followed him down, pressing the gimlet against the same spot. Bobo Shin looked up at her in agonized disbelief.

Then he saw the blade jutting out of Clara's hold, pointing back toward herself. It was the handle she pressed against the Master's rib. "I'm so sorry," she said, pulling back the gimlet. "I didn't mean to surprise you that way, Roshi."

"Not at all." He rose slowly, assisting himself along Clara's calves, thighs, loins. "You are magnificent. You are my every-thing. Where were you just now? Can we go there?"

* * *

"You stink. Move away." Suds shuddered. He was still combing mites and filth out of his whiskers, then looking for something to clean his hands on. There was only Virya and the hard ground.

"You stink too. Hands off."

"I don't like death, Virya. I like life." When he looked at Virya now, he saw her bones, the skull behind her face, her silly breasts jutting out like mud piles from the real Virya—ribs and gristle. So, too, his prick, their buns, and everything they used to think of as themselves.

Back in the bone pit, everything had stuck to them—gristle, bugs, and rot. Sliding in, they had still been drenched from the downpour outside. The lower they went, the easier it got, because the hulks down there had rotted more. The half-gone stiffs were worst, the ones that still had a look you almost had to return; they were at the top. Virya made Suds keep going. It was a shortcut to the City, she said. Bobo Shin's guys went just this way, she said. Keep down, be quiet, she said, don't jostle those bones, and can't you hear the monks—they're close below.

Then the awful lava tube, dark, cold, claustrophobic, inclining up onto the karst. It was impossible to get rid of the stink. Suds yanked at a knot in his beard until he yelped. "I'm going to cut it off."

"Suds, look. What are they doing?"

"Shaking off goo, looks like."

"No, they're fighting."

"Not fighting—war games. Zen wars. Let's go back. How'd they stay so clean? But let's not go back through the bone pit, Virya. Let's go another way."

"You don't mean that. We're practically at the City. Look. It's there."

"Looks like a dump. I don't like it."

"You're *icchantika*, Suds. I give up on you. And stay low."

Chapter Twelve

I inched down until I could spring onto the wet incline below. Above me, No Mind and Pirate, limbs entwined, crept down like a crippled spider. Near the bottom, No Mind dropped him. Pirate fell hard onto his chest and yowled. I kicked him. No Mind jumped down and scrambled out of the way. His legs and arms were so torched that he could barely stand straight. He caught his breath at a safe distance from Pirate.

Angela was climbing down, sure-footed and steady. Somehow she managed to find holds even in the smooth rock toward the bottom of the chute. She never had to spread-eagle across the gap as we had. She just hugged the rock, kept her weight over her feet, and found all the right holds as if by magnetism. The witch had Tao by the balls—and Tenacity on her shoulder.

"Pirate!" She lowered herself onto the rock where Pirate was groaning and clutching the ribs I'd kicked. She glared at No Mind and me.

I glared back. "He tried to kill me. If No Mind hadn't helped me out, I'd be ground beef."

Pirate labored to his knees, then to his feet. "Big Man, he pushed my hand out. I wasn't trying to punch you. You don't know who your friends are."

"That's what I told him, Pirate." No Mind worked his way around to my side. "Only when I said it, it was true, wasn't it Big Man?"

"Looks like it," I said.

Angela held Pirate as if he were his. She worried over his bruises and looked into his eyes to feel his hurt with him. She held him close. "Can you do somethin' about this, Tenacity?"

"Naw, I'm useless at this kind of thing. Them hodags up by our place could fix him easy, especially the wingbacks. Not me. I'm strictly a philosopher and leader of men."

"Well," I said, "it's a straight shot up onto the karst now, isn't it? Thanks for the goo, Angela. Thanks for everything. I guess No Mind and I can stumble up without any more help. You too, Pirate—thank you. You've been a real buddy. You can stick here with your lover or do whatever the hell makes you happy."

Pirate had the nerve to say, "I love you, Big Man, even with all your crap." No Mind snickered, but Pirate didn't mind him. "Didn't you hear yourself up there? You pull the snake up out of the slime, and then you let it slither down again just like you never saw a thing."

"Shut up."

"What's goin' on?" Angela said.

"He thinks you're some chick named Janus."

Angela gasped. She seemed faint. She sat down on the wet rock.

"I don't," I said.

"You act like it, damn it."

"You don't know what you're talking about." I looked at Angela. She was talking to herself. "What in hell is wrong with you?"

"I'm not you! I'm not you!" She was staring into space.

"Where did you get that?" I said. "I've been seeing that crap all over."

"I love you, Big Man. You gotta believe me. I'll just bust if you don't. I come from here. I come down these tubes from the City. I never knew what I was. I wasn't s'posta. 'I'M NOT YOU,' see? That was for *me*. That got put there for *me*.

"I'm rememberin' now. In the City you think with one another's brains. The food you chew tumbles into a thousand stomachs, and at night you dream the dreams of a thousand souls. You feel scared, maybe, for the guy on your left—that's what you do for him—and he pisses for you. We're all inside one another there.

"I'm rememberin'. The City broke me off and sent me out to

fetch you, Big Man. 'I'M NOT YOU,' is what a baby cries when it grunts out between its mama's legs, see, and the mama screams: 'YOU'RE NOT ME!' That's what it's all about.

"Amitabha, I'm rememberin' stuff. When I was fresh out of the City and couldn't think or say a word besides that, I was already thinkin' and sayin', 'I'M NOT YOU!" I scratched it in silt, rock, steamed windows, and styrofoam. Or sometimes it was there for me already: the Catchers said it, or the City dreamed it into somebody else to scrawl somewheres, just for me, to heal me where they broke me off, see, like you stick a sawed-off arm in the fire to seal it.

"So now I'm just me. I swallow my own food and think my own thoughts—till I bring you back with me, Big Man. We'll be like babies scramblin' back into Mama. Ain't that what everybody wants?

"Oh Amitabha, now I remember somethin' else. It's like a flood inside. Amitabha, it's gonna bust me to pieces. I'm rememberin' with somebody else's brains, *but she's me too*. Her name is *Janus*. I'm *Janus*, Big Man, and I'm sorry. I'm so sorry. I love you. I never wanted to leave you. That's why the City picked me to fetch you in."

"She's a hypostat, Big Man," Tenacity said. "Jello's a hypostat... and so are you."

* * *

My mind logjammed. I couldn't begin to think or talk.

The drip turned into a cataract splashing down the chute, pooling at our feet, filling scallops in the wavy rock. Tenacity didn't like it. Every so often, out of his pipe butt, he blasted air so hot it boiled the puddles and made a dry spot around him. Where Angela crouched, the water showered over her. She wouldn't move. She couldn't stop shaking. She couldn't stop crying. Pirate put his arm around her.

The two of them.

"I got a lot of stuff the City wants to tell you, Big Man," she said.

I blurted out, "I'm no hypostat. You're not Janus. What is all this?"

"It's true." Angela's eyes were a perfect counterfeit of sincerity. "It's like Tenacity said. The lot of us is just pieces of stuff. Not one of us is a whole thing. The City's playing all of us like a pipe organ, Big Man, or like them muscles in your arm, muscle against muscle—all for you."

"That's the dharma." Tenacity sizzled on the wet ramp like an overheated radiator. "City's looking for the right chord. Tells this guy this, that guy that, has us all bumping heads—now I know what for: to get you back in, Big Man. That's what we're all about."

Angela took Pirate's hand. "Yeah, Pirate, that's what you're all about too—even if you're a piece of a transcat."

"Damn you, Angela." Pirate pulled his arm away and stood up too fast—he grimaced when he tried to straighten his back. "That's my business."

Tenacity jetted around from one of us to the other. "You one-notes make me laugh. Us whaddayagets are used to being a smorgasbord, but with you it's a goddam Greek Tragedy. Who cares? Angela's a stat of Janus. Pirate's a transcat's toupée. No Mind..." No Mind just stood there with a blank look on his face. "No Mind?"

"Yuh?"

"Lost your buddha nature?"

"Huh?"

Tenacity roared his laughter. "His Voice is gone. City's put him on cruise control. Interesting... Your turn, Big Man..." He sidled up to tag me.

I was getting tired of the little show they were putting on for me. Obviously, all they wanted was to screw up my head and get me out of the picture, so Pirate and Angela, the golden kids, could couple. "I don't want to hear this, Tenacity."

"I know you don't. I know you don't. That's all according to schedule, you dumb oaf. The City's playing you like a hand of canasta. 'I hate torching my brains over gone shit.' Do you know your father's and your mother's names?" He was tagging me, reading me. It was a low blow—I was so mixed up, I couldn't keep him away from my mind. "Think about it, whiz kid. How come you don't got any memories before the Ramp?"

"Stop it."

"You're a missing piece of the City, bub, the block that the masons throwed away. TOO MUCH EGO. STEP ASIDE. YOU'RE HOLDING UP THE LINE. Only now they know they need you. Place is rotting for the dead foresquares jammin' it. They need jissom, *joriki*, and moxie, Big Man. They need Doubt Mass. They need you."

Angela came close to me. She was like a ghost or an angel, glistening in dim cave light. She put her hands on my chest. "Please. I'm s'posta help get you in, Big Man. The City picked what was left of Janus to stat out, I mean, of me, 'cause you loved me. And I love you. I still do."

"Then why did you leave me like that...?" I stepped back—her hands reached after me—then fell to her sides. I turned to Pirate. "Good work. You nearly had me, Pirate. Come on, No Mind. Let's get out onto the karst. Let's leave this crapola underground. I'm going into the City. What about you?"

I took No Mind's arm. We walked up the incline. It got brighter and brighter. Angela, Pirate and Tenacity stayed behind for a moment, then came running after us.

"This is great," Tenacity said. "This is just what I love. See how interesting that meatloaf is? I love his guts. Them hodags is a cow town compared to him. Wait up, pal."

He was kissing my butt with those baby lips; then, before I knew it, I was sitting on him, on that rusted muffler of a body. He had scooted between my legs and risen half a foot; I rode him like a horse. Angela kept calling, "Big Man! Big Man!" I didn't want to slow down. Pirate grumbled and came abreast of us, just as we came in full sight of the cave's mouth.

The daylight was blinding, but we could hear movement out there, metal clashing, people growling and heaving things around. Someone shouted in a thick accent: "Awake! Awake, you devils! Awake!"

Chapter Thirteen

The first-in-line applicant when the screen blew up was a tall woman in a taupe caftan. Fragments of glass mutilated her face. She did not scream. She thought she was being hypodyned. She was in bliss. She thought the billowing smoke was the dissolution of the first skandha of materiality. She thought she was attaining sainthood in the City. She took her sudden blindness to be supra-mundane insight. The pain didn't matter.

She did not understand the pressure against her shoulders and hips. She did not perceive that people were pushing her out of the way of the spreading fires. The popping and exploding through the hypostat lines struck her as molecular events of which she was now becoming aware in her transcendentally attuned state. The hicks and guards who tried to save her failed. The slender pyramid of a transcatalytic bulb was thrown from its housing, and it pierced the woman's left eye all the way into the forebrain, killing her.

Four vannies rushed Control, thinking they could sneak into the City. A few Chevelles pulled chairs up from their rusted floor bolts and hurled them at the guards: "'Not you,' huh? 'Not you,' huh?" More small fires. The guards shook and thumped their radio transmitters. When the smoke got worse, they ran.

Down from the encircling balcony, leaping handrails, parting clumps of applicants as a boning knife cleaves gristle, two super-visors shot through to the turnstile and vaulted over. No one had ever seen them move anything before except their eyes and a pencil.

The enamel on the swinging doors peeled away in a blast of heat from the melting transcatalyzer. The supervisors pushed through. Smoke swelled out. They ducked low. The hypodyne techies in their white jumpsuits were coughing as they crawled toward the exits. One of the supervisors grabbed a technician by the collar. "What happened? What in hell happened?"

"Communication's down. Everything just blew—from inside, from the City end. It's nothing we did. Somebody's bypassing Control. Fucker's on the karst. The City's bristling like a spooked cat."

"Can we still dyne?"

"Lemme go. We gotta get out of here."

"Can we still dyne?"

The techy yanked himself away and was swallowed by low, swirling fumes. For all the supervisor could see, he was alone in eddies of blue smoke. The supervisor groped along the floor, navigating by the seams in the floor tiles. He found a wall, then the right wall, then, by their screeching, the crows in their cage the size of a giant redwood. The dyne barrel would be near.

Now he felt it—the long, flexible tube of optical fibers. He grabbed it with one hand and clutched the cage with the other. With beaks and talons the crows tore at him. They were hypostats: forbidden wisdom, enveloping darkness, and—*yaw, yaw, yaw!*—alarm. Never mind the pain. He fixed the barrel's aim and slid his fingers along the tube until he felt the bump of the console.

In a pinch, there were only four switches to tend—ON, ON, OFF, ON, then wait one second and switch number two to OFF. A bright flash lit the smoke. Then came the sizzle of the residual hypostat, after the birds were jazz—if they were—to place them into the City. Could he hear them now? No. Maybe they had made it through.

Or maybe he was too far gone to hear anything.

* * *

The dyne barrel had been too hot from all the fires to function properly. Only part of the jazz it made of the crows statted down inside the City. Some crow-jazz spilled out into the Saha World.

It condensed like water vapor on dust, when clouds form. Transcat-like, it seeped backwards in time and began to rain, about twelve hours earlier, during the Full Moon Ceremony at the Cave of the Dharma. It trickled at first, then poured, then flooded. Lost rivers roared through underground chambers.

The suburbers had spread their umbrellas against crows and the cawing of crows, a cloudburst of crows that splashed like rain. Rinzai, running after the monks, had sloshed through the black birds' music. The beaks and claws and iridescent feathers of crows had tumbled down the chute over Angela, and she was soaked to the marrow with the sly cock of a crow's head. At the Old On Ramp folks huddled under clammy car-tops while the predatory wisdom of crows smeared their windshields and thundered against rusted metal.

All this was an emergency alarm—Control was burning open. With exquisite subtlety, the City shifted, altering the permeability of its miles of skin. It readied itself for Big Man.

Chapter Fourteen

They looked like angels up there in the light. I still couldn't make them out. I'd been in the night world too long.

Tenacity rocketed out from under me, scorching my thighs as he zoomed into the light. I only dropped a few inches, but I wasn't ready for it. I stumbled to my knees.

Pirate offered me his hand, but I didn't take it. I got up on my own and kept walking toward the mouth of the cave. No Mind and Pirate, each for his own reasons, walked right beside me, and Angela was just a little behind. I felt her there without looking. I always felt where she was... just like Janus. Shut up, mind. Shut up. Shut up. Shut up.

The figures out there began to take shape. The first one I made out was Clara, the vanny bitch, the pretty one, who'd had a shouting match with Angela the night before Pirate and I left the Ramp. As my eyes got used to daylight, I saw her robes, her red hair, her freckles. She had a *rakusu* now, a ceremonial bib like Bobo Shin's. She was standing tall, holding something shiny in her fist. She raised it high over her head...

...And brought it down on Tenacity. There was a sharp clang. Tenacity uttered half a word and dropped to the hard ground like a busted muffler. He rolled a few times, then lay still. I started to run out to help him, but No Mind blocked the way.

No Mind's stupor seemed to have passed. He had jumped in front of me to face Pirate, who was still at my side. "Pirate, you bastard," he said, "you set us up."

Pirate took a swing at him, but I stepped between them and knocked Pirate's fist aside with my forearm. Pirate grabbed my arm and pulled me within biting range.

"Tenacity!" Angela ran out onto the karst to help the little guy.

That's when I saw the rest of them, six or seven mean-looking priest types with knives. I recognized their chief, though he

105

wasn't wearing his *rakusu*; it was Bobo Shin Roshi, one of the crystal-set honchos the vannies sucked up to. There was a little boy with them, too, a freckly kid I'd seen hanging around with Angela in the old days. Pirate pushed me away and ran after Angela.

"Right." No Mind watched Pirate fly at the monks. "He pretends to fight them. He lures you out, Big Man, and then he and his pals get you."

Pirate's gang put on a convincing show. While Clara picked up Tenacity to hurl him out of the way, the other thugs made for Angela. Pirate picked up a rock and stepped in. They all started swinging. Pirate kicked and jabbed, outmaneuvering most of them. They outnumbered him, but they were hysterical and fought stupidly, all at once on a single front, so he could pick them off as they got in one another's way.

Pirate stood between the monks and Angela. He held them off while she bent over Tenacity, cooing and fussing. Clara seemed to be waiting for the little monks to clear the way to Angela. Bobo Shin was a ways back, screaming, "Kill! Kill!" It gave me the chills. At the same time, if it wasn't a mirage—off by themselves across the karst, I thought I saw the weak, bearded hick I'd kicked out of the Blue Plymouth Hotel and his gristly woman. They were charging toward the City. They kept turning to see if anybody was coming after them—and stumbling over their own feet.

Sometimes, at right angles to everything that's happening, you get a kind of a thought. It can be a year's worth of a thought, but you never miss a beat. You think the whole thing between one breath and the next. I thought:

#

Is this what you have to go through to get into the City: turn into a beast, break every precept, cover yourself with filth inside and outside? Do you have to become a bloody murderer to be a Cityzen? Then...
#

"...Gaaaa!" I charged Pirate from behind.

"Go," No Mind yelled. He ran along—to back me up, I figured. I had to hand it to him. He wasn't a big guy. He wasn't a scrapper. But, unlike Pirate, he was there for me. And when he got that look in his eyes—whether it was buddha mind or devils, I don't care—he had enough *joriki*, enough inner electricity, to rush a garrison.

From behind, I pulled Pirate's shoulder back with my right hand. The rock he'd been wielding jerked from his grasp and hit the ground. I've never seen a human being look so surprised. I was about to put him to sleep with my left, when something yanked my arms back.

It was No Mind. He had jumped up on my back and was locking my arms for all he was worth. The monks circled the three of us, me immobile, Pirate so buffaloed he didn't know which end was up, and No Mind grunting to hang onto me—a losing bet. I pumped my arms and he fell away like rotted plaster. Then he dropped back: to join the monks. Suddenly Pirate and I were on the same side, defending our lives against Bobo Shin's crew.

They were all around us and closing in. Clara's path to Angela was clear. The vanny brat Rinzai looked on like a salt pillar, paralyzed; only his eyes moved. Bobo Shin was so happy now, he just pretzeled his legs, took on the dark look, and did zazen.

Pirate crouched low, his arms stretched out threateningly toward the monks. He menaced them, feinting and lunging. They scored his hands with their knives; he dripped blood but hardly noticed. "Do you see it now, Big Man?"

I pressed my back against Pirate's and turned with him, keeping them at bay. "I don't see anything."

"Then look over there." He whirled, to face me toward Angela. I could see her with Tenacity, past the little monks. Clara stood over her, holding the knife almost playfully now. Pirate pressed the back of his head against mine, and his voice hummed through me: "This is what you did, Big Man, while I was trying to hold them back. You cut me off, and the vanny chick got through. You've killed Angela, you poor jerk."

* * *

"*Kill! Kill!*" Rinzai could not block his voice out any longer. "*Hear the Voice of the City. Kill, Rinzai. Kill Angela.*"

He picked up a fallen knife. Clara's arm and torso were pumping up and down like a piston. With each thrust, her gimlet came up redder. Angela still fought. Guarding Tenacity, she held onto Clara's robe and gradually pulled her down.

Rinzai moved toward them.

* * *

Pirate gave an ear to Big Man's whimper: "Why are they doing this, Pirate?" *As if I knew.* Pirate thought. *Kick now: hyahh!* "We gotta get to her," Big Man told him. "We gotta get to Angela." *A little bit late, wasn't it?* "Maybe we can work over that way. Just keep circling, see, inching left. Stay with me, Pirate. Stay with me. Is she bleeding…? Watch out." *Hyahh!*

It was a plan: keep circling, inching left. The monks wouldn't rush them. The monks were just waiting for Clara to slaughter Angela, so she could come over and help them murder Big Man and Pirate. The two men could stall them, but they couldn't do much damage.

Pirate didn't dare look in Angela's direction too long, or they might close in. He had to use his eyes like bayonets, poking and threatening. Now and then a kick—*Hyahh!*—like that one.

Keep circling, inching left. Pirate kept his eyes moving, his head bobbing, holding the monks at bay. The adrenalin rush of combat so wakened him that it was as if his mind had pushed out an extra chamber where thoughts echoed despite the crush of activity.

What was he worth? *Nothing,* came the thought. He didn't even belong to himself. Nothing he did came from him. He was like a butt when a person squats to shit: it just went through him. If the transcat shimmied, he shook. Even this thought was some transcat's jazz. He was worth about a handful of couch-grass chaff.

Hyahh! That little guy wouldn't stop to fix his robes again.

When Pirate felt Big Man's sweaty shoulders pressed against his, was it the transcat feeling it, really? If that was true—and Pirate thought it was—then death would be interesting. The transcat would keep right on feeling, without the lie of Pirate inbetween, just as when you tore off a man's finger, there were plenty more things he could make do with. *I'm less important to my transcat than a finger is to a man.*

Hyahh! Hyahh! Keep circling, inching left. The monks were backing off a little—a new tactic. They had finally figured out that there was no hurry; time was on their side.

Hyahh! That one was just to blow off steam. *Look at the cowards sag back.* Pirate could see Angela clearly now, holding onto Clara's calves. She was a mess of blood.

What was Big Man blubbering about this time? "...Of course I love her. I love her, Pirate. Somewhere inside me, I always knew she was hooked up with Janus. Don't you see, that's why I couldn't let her near me. It hurt too much. And then there's the holes. What do you do with the holes...?"

Big Man, Pirate thought, *I sympathize, but is this the moment...? Never mind—there probably won't be another one.*

"...Holes in your memory, holes in your feelings where something's supposed to be—what do you do with them?" *Hyahh!*

Shut up, Big Man. I don't want to talk about my holes.

"I'm some jazz the City trashed, Pirate. It rings true. I always felt like half a man."

Keep circling, inching left. They were practically there. Why couldn't Big Man shut up? It was working. *Swing left. Hyahh! Hyahh!* Clara was before them. If they could just push through *right now...*

Help me, Big Man. I'm cut. No Mind cut me, damn him. I'm cut.

* * *

Bobo Shin had uncrossed his legs and was coming to cinch the matter for Clara. A strategic kick to Angela's head, he thought, would do the trick. Carefully skirting the deadly circle around Pirate and Big Man, Bobo Shin came alongside Rinzai. "You're a good boy. Stay close to me. Protect your Roshi. Careful of the witch."

Rinzai bit him.

"You little shit-sucking devil, what do you think you're doing? Don't you know it's breaking a cardinal precept to even give a priest a mean look? You might as well bite the arse of Shakyamuni Buddha himself." Rinzai kicked Bobo Shin's knee. The Roshi danced and fell.

Rinzai's head throbbed: *"Kill Angela. Kill the icchantika."*

"No!" Rinzai dived into Clara from behind. He grabbed her legs and pushed at the hamstrings. She collapsed straight down. Her knees hit; then the heels of her hands slammed down, as she reached back to break her fall. Rinzai scooted out of the way. Blinking blood out of her right eye—her slashed forehead oozed thick, dark blood—Angela grabbed the gimlet and held it against Clara's throat. Close by, a hubbub: Big Man and Pirate had managed to work nearer—a desperate plan, as likely to hurt as to help—and they were trying to break out.

"Help me, Big Man. I'm cut. No Mind cut me, damn him. I'm cut."

Angela turned to look. Clara dropped to one elbow, falling away from the knife, and with her freed hand she clutched Angela's wrist and pushed it away. Angela pressed the knife toward Clara. It hovered between them.

Rinzai rolled on the ground, holding his ears and pinching his eyes shut. The vengeance of his Voice was terrific. His mind could not hold its thunder.

In the circle of knives, Big Man turned and knelt to protect Pirate. One of the monks attacked him from behind. The monk looped his *obi*, a broad black sash, around Big Man's neck, and twisted. Big Man yelped and gurgled. When he tried to fight back, half a dozen knives cut into him.

Big Man and Pirate neutralized, No Mind stepped behind Angela and took her head in the crook of his arm. She made a piteous sound, soon muffled. The knife was Clara's again.

For the first time since before the suburb, Bobo Shin heard the crystal-set Voice. He was flooded with a feeling of profound gratitude. He would have done one hundred and eight prostrations had the situation seemed less tense. He performed three or four anyway, then did what the Voice asked him to. He called Mukan away from the circle.

Mukan came running. He stopped twenty or thirty feet from Bobo Shin and performed his obeisance. "Master!"

"The boy Rinzai is *icchantika*, oh monk. He impedes the work of the City. He does not exist in reality. Kill him."

Mukan looked over at Rinzai writhing on the ground, screaming without sound. He regarded his knife. "How has this tool fallen to me?" Mukan thought—the old testing question. Then he threw it. It struck Bobo Shin in his neck, just above the carotid artery. Bobo Shin lowered his chin to feel what small thing could have struck him there—a pebble set flying, perhaps, or else a horsefly? The knife sliced down—and he fell dead almost instantly, collapsing like a magician's sheet, the dove underneath it vanished.

Before anyone but he could understand what had happened, Mukan returned to the circle; with three or four strategic blows to his astonished brother monks, Mukan freed Big Man. Big Man struck Clara hard in the back of the neck. She fell senseless. No Mind let go Angela and ran.

Big Man started to pursue him, when Angela rasped, "Pirate!" Turning, he saw the monks drag Pirate away over Mukan's prone body. Mukan's arms and legs splayed out in ugly angles. He was not moving.

One of the monks followed behind the others, walking backwards, facing Big Man and brandishing his knife. "Come at us, and we'll butcher him. Life and death are illusions to us." His voice cracked. A few monks wheezed hysterically, half-sobbing, as they dragged Pirate along. His wrists were bound behind his back now.

"Your teacher's dead," Big Man trumpeted. "Where do you think you'll take my man? What are you going to do with him? Why don't you give it up?"

"I don't know. I don't know." The monk clutched the gimlet and so tightened the muscles in his arm that it shivered up and down like a jack hammer.

The monks stopped. When Pirate tried to speak; one of them pulled a *zagu* from his sleeve—a cloth he threw down for prostrations, and he stuffed part of it in Pirate's mouth. Another monk bound it shut and held Pirate's chin back, exposing the stubbly, soft skin underneath...

Suddenly, the air seemed to darken and gel. The slaughterhouse stench was swept away by a rush of ozone. It was cold. From the mouth of the cave hodags streamed, stampeded, thundered, flew.

They were everywhere at once. A gelatinous willy engulfed No Mind and slithered toward Angela, with No Mind gooed inside. When a whaddayaget's tail knotted one monk's wrists like a tangling vine, the others fled. Twenty nightmares pursued them across the karst. 'Scope rode the spined birds, shouting directions from the air.

Fine shadows as of acacia or hemlock leaves—and the

sensation of vague hope mixed with dim, unnamable under-standing—fell across Angela, and her bleeding stopped. "That'll be Foxhole," Tenacity croaked. He clanked to his plated feet, wobbled a little, then shook off some rust. "It's about time." He rolled backward to stop Angela from kissing him on his baby cheeks—"Wait."

"Tenacity, what is it, ya sweetheart?"

"Transcat."

Then she felt it too.

Chapter Fifteen

Suds's teeth chattered. Virya mumbled pidgin Sanskrit and chewed her lip all bloody.

It looked like a quarter-mile-high cube of flesh, cavernous, as if worm-eaten, riddled with flashing pin lights, whole sections glowing or dimming, glistening with moisture, then drying and becoming dull as juice slicked a different section, electric to the touch, pulsing erratically with accumulations of tiny, erratic bursts, waves of sound like swept rain, like radio static, scanning for a station. Occasionally, as Suds and Virya stood gazing, they were teased by a transient, nearly identifiable impression: a whiff of ether, a burning sensation and the taste of fennel, someone else's memory, an urgent, indecipherable plea, the heat of a look from some unknown source, words forming and fading like rain sizzling on a hot engine, like spring snow, like sunlight in a jar, like the smell of gasoline, like the shadow of a passing cloud, a half-remembered name, another life, the telephone number of a childhood address, a phrase from a song in a foreign language heard from a passing train—though one feels that one under-stands—and like all things one lacks the stamina to comprehend or the swiftness to run alongside.

Suds touched the City here and there as he walked its perimeter, and images streamed into him like blood through an IV: corpses in drawers, a clump of worms in a bait can, maggot-infested droppings, one's own feces found teeming and tunneled with gleaming worms, ghoulish horrors, and, at the same time, interloping visions of a gone century: businessmen's lunch at a buzzing Manhattan diner, commuter trains to Tokyo replacing red blood cells in a sleeper's arteries, the heart a roundhouse for the intercity locals, caffeine, caffeine, television roulette, a big City welfare building *cum* VD clinic *cum* stock exchange, wildmen leaping like popcorn from sizzling oil to bid on penny stocks knocking against the steamy Pyrex pot lid, leaving drippy grease marks—you take it off the burner, remove the lid, and a dozen more kernels explode across the room.

Shivering and grabbing at the air, Suds skidded backwards on his buttocks. "Amitabha, this heap is the City? It smells like manure. It looks like a big hemorrhoid."

"That's your worldly eye, Suds." Virya threw up—just once, everything. She wiped sweat from her forehead and took a deep breath. "That's better. That's a lot better. That's all my impurities gone now."

"Screw that. We've been lied to. This place is a dump. This is what they've been bleeding us for? This is what they do zazen for?"

"When a pickpocket meets a holy man, he only sees the holy man's wallet. This thing is Nirvana. Let's push in, Sudsy. I bet we melt right into it. I bet it just takes away all your troubles, just like that."

"It bounced me back like a high power line."

"Just press on through, honey. Hold my hand. We'll do it together. Don't be afraid to die. I know it, I feel it—if we brave that barrier, it's just like passing Control. That's the last ego barrier, Sudsy. We've got to prove our trust in Buddha Amitabha, and then we'll be free. Come on."

Suds gritted his teeth—and held Virya's hand. His shoulders were up to his ears. He squeezed his whiskered face up like a prune. His stomach knotted, his toes bunched into the balls of his feet as if they were strapped into bindings. Suds closed his eyes. Slowly, he moved forward with Virya, she resolute, he using every remaining second to complete his tally of grievances against her and life generally.

His skin tingled. The follicles of all his bodily hair prickled, as when the charged skin of a balloon passed over it. Suds and Virya moved slowly enough this time to sense each gradation: the tingle, the prickle, the buzz as of a limb un-numbed, and then the pain, like walking into an iron maiden and shutting the door from inside.

* * *

The whaddayas scooped the fleeing monks into their claws, pockets, teeth, anuses, mouths—and memories the shape and toughness of cattle cars. They crowed victory as they paraded their captives back toward the caves. En route, they collected No Mind, jelloed, and Clara, woozy, into their main column. Then they felt the transcategorical buckling the ether between their bones.

The transcategorical whipped its great tail. The On Ramp rippled and split. It stopped raining. It started raining.

In the sudden stillness, Pirate sighed. His wrists were still tied behind his back, his mouth stuffed and bound shut. He lay on the ground where the monks had dropped him. He was staring up at the sky. Parts of Big Man occluded his sky for a moment—Big Man's head, his shoulder, his hand on Pirate's cheek. There was a troubled look in Big Man's eyes. Big Man's mouth was moving, and Pirate heard sounds coming out, but he didn't know what they meant. For the moment, he had forgotten that the sounds were supposed to refer to something.

He was not on the karst. He was in a basin on Mercury, many years hence—there and elsewhere past naming. The thing on the karst was dead skin. It was what he had seen the day Suds had tattooed "Party down!" around his navel and Pirate had ceased to do zazen. Only now he saw it without bitterness. He had no ego to grate against the transcat's ego. Falling, bleeding, dragging— somewhere, it had dropped away. Everything was simply factual. Pirate was dead skin.

The transcat shivered through the space-time of the karst, the City, the century, and was gone.

"Pirate? Pirate? Can you hear me, buddy?"

"Mmmffggghh!"

"What?" Big Man ungagged him.

Pirate spat out the bunched cloth. "I said, go take care of Angela, you ugly sonuvabitch. I'm fine. Just untie me first... Don't you ever brush your teeth?"

Big Man kissed him loudly on the mouth and ran to Angela.

"Hey, my wrists!" But Pirate didn't really care. The sky was clear, as it always was above the karst. The sun was setting slowly into the ring of mountains. He didn't know which one he was—the sun, the sky, the mountains, the plain, or one of the mammalian bipeds lying on the earth, two of them dead. Maybe he was one of the live ones scurrying about, or just their sound, or all or none of them. It didn't seem important. He was sweetly tired, and it felt good just to breathe.

Big Man took Angela's hands. "You're all right."

Tenacity hopped to Angela's shoulder and skewered Big Man with a squint. "Tag!" he said. "You're all right too, beefsteak. The madness has lifted. The heart has cleared. God's in his heaven. Is that what all this bullshit was for?"

Angela said, "That's what all this bullshit was for. I love you, Big Man."

"I know it, darling," said Big Man.

"I'm gonna puke now," Tenacity said. "Don't let it distract you. Humans just do that to me sometimes. Excuse me." He jetted to the parade of whaddayagets. "Give me one of them monks, you astigmatisms. I want someone to vomit on."

#

I exist. I exist. I am the Lord your God, who brought you out of the land of Egypt, the House of Bondage, with a strong arm and a mighty hand,
#

Tenacity vomited. "There's an eloquent upchuck for you," he gasped between heaves, wiping chunks of syllables from something like a mouth.

#

I am called, "I Am That I Am." I exist, I exist, and you do not, except in so far as I breathe into you the breath of my life, and when it is withdrawn, you are no more. I revealed myself to you in the flame in Midian, on Mount Horeb, and to men and women of the inner eye in countless other places with countless other names. I am Buddha Dharma. I am Allah. I am Ahurah Mazda.

#

The monk he was clutching had nearly made it out of his robes. Covered in Tenacity's horrifying vomitus, he screamed and scrambled, face stretched like an exploding gum wad. Tenacity told him, "Nowadays, they call it 'the City.' It's using us all to whip up *joriki*. It's using us one against the other, like pairs of muscles, see? Agonist, antagonist: that's how you get things done. The City makes Angela leave and come back with the oaf here—excuse me while I wipe—makes No Mind try to sow distrust, makes your roshi try to kill Angela or Rinzai, everybody ganging up…"

#

I exist when the City requires it. I am heat lightning, I am a sudden breeze, I am a bubble in a stream, but while I exist I am all powerful. All beings are my skin and my extremities—nothing more. You are my extremity. You are my fingertip, my tongue tip, my cock, my cunt, or my eye, or the sclera of my eye. Let me, then, save the City, my City.

#

"Anybody got some coke syrup? Dramamine? I can't keep throwing up like this. Big Man, you're a firecracker in a trashcan, and the City is lighting you and clapping on the lid. It's all to make you blow and blow big, to blow you inside the City." He burped loudly, and the monk at last shook loose and ran away. Tenacity staggered back toward Big Man. "Consider yourself tagged."

Big Man stared into Angela's eyes. "You're hurting," he said. "It's Janus in me. We gotta enter the City, Big Man. Tenacity is right. It's what I saw in No Mind's eyes back there in the cave. That's what it's all for. We're bendin' for it. We're pushin' for it. We're what quickens it all again. You still wanna, don'tcha?"

"You're talking to a piece of the goddam City, darling. I've got Doubt Mass like a black hole. I've got *joriki* like a supernova. Show me the City, Angela."

* * *

Rinzai rode on Angela's back. Vacantly, he watched the City loom larger as they approached it. He hadn't spoken since seeing Mukan's corpse. Rinzai's face was white, and there was a hollow look in his eyes. When Tenacity japed, he didn't laugh. When Pirate chucked him under the chin, he neither smiled nor frowned.

"Yeah, the City reamed him between the ears," was Tenacity's tag. "Listen, I could hot rod him back to the whaddayas. They could fix him quick, once them monks is cooked and eaten."

"Just wait till we get in," Angela said, "back in, I mean."

They advanced toward the City. The volcanic earth was hard and hot. They skirted sinkholes and sudden pits but the swells and barrows they marched straight over, eyes magnetized to the dark mound. It loomed larger and larger before them against the dwindling, rosy light. Venus was already pricking through. Jupiter appeared between the saw teeth of the hills.

Big Man led them. His pace quickened as the edges of the City came into focus. "It's a place," he said. "That's what I can't get over. It's an actual place."

Angela shifted Rinzai on her back—dead weight. "Don't think that way, Big Man. That thing is just how it looks from here."

"No. That's the City. Come on." He leapt forward, still holding Angela's hand. Their arms pulled taut, like a stretched cord, and Angela's hand fell away. Big Man vaulted across a small swallet and broke toward the City. He galloped straight ahead, enjoying the wind of his own movement, then slowed and came to a stop a hundred yards before the thing.

The smell of it stopped him—sickly sweet, rotting. Daylight was disappearing, and the moon, just past full, had not yet risen above the mountains, but he thought he saw maggots swarming on the City's surface. Dreams swelled out at him, bad dreams, chaotic stories with broken logic. They badgered and sucked till his mind, like the City, teemed with maggots.

Angela was holding his hand again. She had put Rinzai down. Pirate stood behind, shushing Tenacity. "Do you hear it, Big Man?" Angela said.

"This is the City?"

"It was. You gotta go in. It changes now. You're the only one who can turn it around, see? You're the brick the maker threw away, the thing that's needed in the end. Make the rot into fertilizer, Big Man. Grow flowers."

"Why couldn't I come in through Control?"

"You can eat stuff through your mouth and gut. You can make your food into a part of you the same as all the other parts. But if you need something really new, a new heart, a new brain, you have to open up the chest, the skull. You have to cut. You have to hurt and bleed."

"This isn't enlightenment," Big Man said. "This isn't the buddha dharma. This isn't what I've been doing zazen for."

"Yes, it is. This is the perfect City the old guys made. Only thing is, as soon as you stat it, it changes. There's always somethin' missin'. And you're the missin' thing, Big Man."

"It smells bad."

"In a minute it won't."

"You're still my picture-window girl, aren't you, Janus?"

Tenacity bit Big Man's heel. "Punch in, you dumb beefsteak. You came this far. Don't say good-bye either. I'll see you in the funny papers."

"Good-bye, Tenacity," he said.

Pirate and Tenacity watched them walk toward the City. At last Rinzai looked up—"Angela!" She didn't hear him. Big Man and Angela were very close to the City now, their bodies aglow with strange electricity. Rinzai broke forward, but Pirate held him.

Rinzai began to cry. "They're flowing in—just like water."

"Yeah, that's it." Tenacity nuzzled him, then jetted back. "They're home now, kiddo."

Rinzai wrapped his arms around Pirate and held on tight. "Pirate—take care of me?"

For a brief moment the sky brightened—zodiacal light—then darkness fell.

* * *

"Climb down, Virya. Climb down, damn it all to hell. I said, climb down." The hole down to the bone-pit passage was only one-person wide. They were tired from running over each other, yank and leapfrog, from the City. Their skin was seared, their nerves shattered.

"Wait a minute, Suds. What was that?"

"Amitabha! A busted muffler just shot by."

"A what?"

"It just shot by and went back up into the caves, so help me God... Will you climb down?"

Virya chinned up out of the hole. "Something's going on."

Suds swore and stamped his foot, but something was going on. A stiff wind blew against them from the City. They squinted and huddled against it. Like tumbleweed and road debris, dreams grazed them, smacked them, stuck in their cuffs, tangled into Suds's beard, and made Virya's eyes tear.

"Is it a transcat?" Suds asked.

"Uh uh. It's the City. Something's going on."

"I don't like it."

Bent low to avoid the push of the wind, Pirate was walking toward them, out of the darkness, from the direction of the City. Rinzai hopped and scuttled along.

"Hey!" Virya called. "Hey! Hey! Pirate, did they get in?"

"Yeah." Pirate didn't slow down. He was walking on past them.

"Wait up. Why didn't you go in?" said Virya.

"Why didn't *you*?"

Virya shouted against the wind, "We could've, Pirate. We almost did. We will, too, only not now. We gotta train more. More zazen. What about you?"

"I'm where I belong... Come on, Rinzai. Stay close to me. I'll teach you how to cook couch grass. I got it all worked out."

Suds was grumbling again. The wind was cold. A stray crow winged and squawked, unequal to the dark, lost among dripstone columns, colliding into them, losing feathers. "Let's climb down, Virya, for Amitabha's sakes."

She started climbing in, then stopped halfway and called to Pirate, "Hey, if you're going back through the Dharma Cave, we got a shortcut here, Pirate."

He didn't look back. He hugged Rinzai as they walked toward the mouth of the cave, then down the incline to the chute, where the cataract had dwindled to a thin stream. There was no wind here, but they were up to their knees in water, and there was a hard climb up.

END

Contemporary culture has eliminated both the concept of the public and the figure of the intellectual. Former public spaces – both physical and cultural – are now either derelict or colonized by advertising. A cretinous anti-intellectualism presides, cheerled by expensively educated hacks in the pay of multinational corporations who reassure their bored readers that there is no need to rouse themselves from their interpassive stupor. The informal censorship internalized and propagated by the cultural workers of late capitalism generates a banal conformity that the propaganda chiefs of Stalinism could only ever have dreamt of imposing. Zer0 Books knows that another kind of discourse – intellectual without being academic, popular without being populist – is not only possible: it is already flourishing, in the regions beyond the striplit malls of so-called mass media and the neurotically bureaucratic halls of the academy. Zer0 is committed to the idea of publishing as a making public of the intellectual. It is convinced that in the unthinking, blandly consensual culture in which we live, critical and engaged theoretical reflection is more important than ever before.

ZERO BOOKS

If this book has helped you to clarify an idea, solve a problem or extend your knowledge, you may like to read more titles from Zero Books. Recent bestsellers are:

Capitalist Realism Is there no alternative?
Mark Fisher
An analysis of the ways in which capitalism has presented itself as the only realistic political-economic system.
Paperback: November 27, 2009 978-1-84694-317-1 $14.95 £7.99.
eBook: July 1, 2012 978-1-78099-734-6 $9.99 £6.99.

The Wandering Who? A study of Jewish identity politics
Gilad Atzmon
An explosive unique crucial book tackling the issues of Jewish Identity Politics and ideology and their global influence.
Paperback: September 30, 2011 978-1-84694-875-6 $14.95 £8.99.
eBook: September 30, 2011 978-1-84694-876-3 $9.99 £6.99.

Clampdown Pop-cultural wars on class and gender
Rhian E. Jones
Class and gender in Britpop and after, and why 'chav' is a feminist issue.
Paperback: March 29, 2013 978-1-78099-708-7 $14.95 £9.99.
eBook: March 29, 2013 978-1-78099-707-0 $7.99 £4.99.

The Quadruple Object
Graham Harman
Uses a pack of playing cards to present Harman's metaphysical system of fourfold objects, including human access, Heidegger's indirect causation, panpsychism and ontography.
Paperback: July 29, 2011 978-1-84694-700-1 $16.95 £9.99.

Weird Realism Lovecraft and Philosophy
Graham Harman
As Hölderlin was to Martin Heidegger and Mallarmé to Jacques
Derrida, so is H.P. Lovecraft to the Speculative Realist philoso-
phers.
Paperback: September 28, 2012 978-1-78099-252-5 $24.95 £14.99.
ebook: September 28, 2012 978-1-78099-907-4 $9.99 £6.99.

Sweetening the Pill or How We Got Hooked on Hormonal Birth
Control
Holly Grigg-Spall
Is it really true? Has contraception liberated or oppressed
women?
Paperback: September 27, 2013 978-1-78099-607-3 $22.95 £12.99.
ebook: September 27, 2013 978-1-78099-608-0 $9.99 £6.99.

Why Are We The Good Guys? Reclaiming Your Mind From The
Delusions Of Propaganda
David Cromwell
A provocative challenge to the standard ideology that Western
power is a benevolent force in the world.
Paperback: September 28, 2012 978-1-78099-365-2 $26.95 £15.99.
ebook: September 28, 2012 978-1-78099-366-9 $9.99 £6.99.

The Truth about Art Reclaiming quality
Patrick Doorly
The book traces the multiple meanings of art to their various
sources, and equips the reader to choose between them.
Paperback: August 30, 2013 978-1-78099-841-1 $32.95 £19.99.

Bells and Whistles More Speculative Realism
Graham Harman
In this diverse collection of sixteen essays, lectures, and inter-
views Graham Harman lucidly explains the principles of

Speculative Realism, including his own object-oriented philosophy.
Paperback: November 29, 2013 978-1-78279-038-9 $26.95 £15.99.
eBook: November 29, 2013 978-1-78279-037-2 $9.99 £6.99.

Towards Speculative Realism: Essays and Lectures Essays and Lectures
Graham Harman
These writings chart Harman's rise from Chicago sportswriter to co founder of one of Europe's most promising philosophical movements: Speculative Realism.
Paperback: November 26, 2010 978-1-84694-394-2 $16.95 £9.99.
eBook: January 1, 1970 978-1-84694-603-5 $9.99 £6.99.

Meat Market Female flesh under capitalism
Laurie Penny
A feminist dissection of women's bodies as the fleshy fulcrum of capitalist cannibalism, whereby women are both consumers and consumed.
Paperback: April 29, 2011 978-1-84694-521-2 $12.95 £6.99.
eBook: May 21, 2012 978-1-84694-782-7 $9.99 £6.99.

Translating Anarchy The Anarchism of Occupy Wall Street
Mark Bray
An insider's account of the anarchists who ignited Occupy Wall Street.
Paperback: September 27, 2013 978-1-78279-126-3 $26.95 £15.99.
eBook: September 27, 2013 978-1-78279-125-6 $6.99 £4.99.

One Dimensional Woman
Nina Power
Exposes the dark heart of contemporary cultural life by examining pornography, consumer capitalism and the ideology of women's work.

Paperback: November 27, 2009 978-1-84694-241-9 $14.95 £7.99.
eBook: July 1, 2012 978-1-78099-737-7 $9.99 £6.99.

Dead Man Working
Carl Cederstrom, Peter Fleming
An analysis of the dead man working and the way in which capital is now colonizing life itself.
Paperback: May 25, 2012 978-1-78099-156-6 $14.95 £9.99.
eBook: June 27, 2012 978-1-78099-157-3 $9.99 £6.99.

Unpatriotic History of the Second World War
James Heartfield
The Second World War was not the Good War of legend. James Heartfield explains that both Allies and Axis powers fought for the same goals - territory, markets and natural resources.
Paperback: September 28, 2012 978-1-78099-378-2 $42.95 £23.99.
eBook: September 28, 2012 978-1-78099-379-9 $9.99 £6.99.

Find more titles at www.zero-books.net